*A Candlelight
Ecstasy Romance*®

"I THOUGHT I'D GO CRAZY WHEN YOU DROPPED OUT OF SIGHT," ADAM SAID SOFTLY.

He kissed her with a sweetness that almost made her forget his betrayal.

"Your book," Hester said, turning her head.

"Did you like it?"

"It was well written, the characterizations were strong. . . . I hated it!"

"Hated it?" He didn't sound as if he believed her.

"Everything we did, everything we felt, you used it all."

"Because it was so important to me."

"But the end of our story was nothing like the book!"

"The end of our story hasn't been written yet, not since I've found you again."

CANDLELIGHT ECSTASY ROMANCES®

A NOVEL AFFAIR

Barbara Andrews

A CANDLELIGHT ECSTASY ROMANCE®

Published by
Dell Publishing Co., Inc.
1 Dag Hammarskjold Plaza
New York, New York 10017

Dell ® TM 681510, Dell Publishing Co., Inc.
Candlelight Ecstasy Romance®, 1,203,540, is a registered
trademark of Dell Publishing Co., Inc., New York, New York.

ISBN: 0-440-16079-0

Printed in the United States of America
First printing—March 1985

*To Dave and Doe DoBell,
great friends who shared
a madrigal evening with us.*

Warren and Barbara Andrews

To Our Readers:

We have been delighted with your enthusiastic response to Candlelight Ecstasy Romances®, and we thank you for the interest you have shown in this exciting series.

In the upcoming months we will continue to present the distinctive sensuous love stories you have come to expect only from Ecstasy. We look forward to bringing you many more books from your favorite authors and also the very finest work from new authors of contemporary romantic fiction.

As always, we are striving to present the unique, absorbing love stories that you enjoy most—books that are more than ordinary romance. Your suggestions and comments are always welcome. Please write to us at the address below.

Sincerely,

The Editors
Candlelight Romances
1 Dag Hammarskjold Plaza
New York, New York 10017

CHAPTER ONE

Earmuffs were sold out in the mall stores, which wasn't surprising; many of the young women on campus were wearing them this blustery January. Hester had survived twenty-eight frigid, snowy winters, most of them in her home state of Maine, without a pair of furry ear coverings, but she was still mildly disappointed. Ms. Paine was one instructor at Halsted College who was willing to learn from her students, especially if it meant being fashionably warm during a Wisconsin cold spell.

The bookstore tempted her, as it always did, although she'd put herself on a strict budget to save money for doctoral-level courses at the University of Wisconsin during her summer break. A single woman could live comfortably on an instructor's salary in the town of Vienne, but a summer in Madison would be a financial drain. Still, she couldn't resist a quick glance at the new arrivals, hard-cover books prominently displayed at the front of the store where shoppers could see them from the concourse. One cover caught her attention and held it: *The Farewell Rock* by Adam Smith-Woodham.

The scene on the dust jacket was dramatic, a jagged rock and a pair of lovers silhouetted against an orange and pink sunset, but the artwork had nothing to do with Hester's stunned reaction. Adam had finally written another book.

It was inevitable that an author of his stature would publish again, but she couldn't believe how painful it was to stumble on his new book without warning. Upset with herself, she hurried away, darting into the nearest refuge, a health food store. The high display shelves and narrow aisles gave her a temporary hiding place while she tried to compose herself, pretending to vacillate between selecting salted or unsalted rice cakes.

After two and a half years in her own personal wilderness, she'd been so sure Adam was out of her system. How could seeing his name on a new book jolt her like a kick to the solar plexus?

She went through the motions of purchasing a plastic bag of the round rice cakes, hardly aware of what she was doing, telling herself it was idiotic to run away from a book display. No one in Vienne had the slightest suspicion that she knew Adam Smith-Woodham. Her colleagues in the English department would be floored if they knew the truth: that the award-winning, best-selling novelist had once loved Hester Paine, starry-eyed graduate student. Unfortunately the distinguished visiting lecturer had had a wife and maybe still did.

There was no money in this month's budget for expensive hard-cover novels. She'd wait for the paperback or put her name on the list to reserve a library copy, but it didn't cost anything to read the blurb. Much against her better judgment, Hester returned to the bookstore and picked up a copy of *The Farewell Rock*, looking first at the author's picture on the back cover. The photographer had taken it at Adam's beach house on the Maine coast, the cluttered little cottage where she'd said good-bye to him. The novelist, dressed in white cotton pants and a dark, bulky pullover, was leaning against a rocky outcrop at the edge of a sandy strip. His hair was unruly, whipped by the ocean wind, but she could almost feel the sandy coarseness of it under her fingers. He was smiling, but not too broadly, his whole pose artfully nonchalant. Adam hated to stand still; he must have seethed with impatience while the photographer fussed with his camera. But Adam wouldn't be rude, not even to a cameraman who insisted on a long, tedious series of shots. He was a perfectionist himself and would tolerate any artist's attention to detail, understanding it because he insisted on polishing and repolishing his prose far beyond the demands of his editor or reading public.

Hester knew all this about the man and more, but what did she really know? Grimly she turned to the inside flap of the dust jacket, slowly reading a synopsis of the plot: "At the peak of his career, Daniel Marvis feels the whole fabric of his life slowly disintegrating."

Not a very inspired story line, Hester thought, hoping Adam hadn't written a moody autobiographical treatise, five hundred pages of humorless self-pity. It was her least favorite theme for a novel, and it hurt to think the man she'd once loved would do that to readers who'd waited so long for another of his books.

Anxious to get rid of the book and the memories it was evoking, she jabbed it down on the metal stand that held one copy upright on a pile of others, tearing the dust jacket from the bottom to the middle. A stock clerk stacking books on the other side of the display looked up in surprise at the tearing sound.

"I'll buy it, of course," Hester mumbled, hurrying to the counter with the damaged merchandise.

At home in her three-room apartment, one of five in a rambling frame house built for a large family at the turn of the century, Hester laid aside the novel, doggedly reminding herself that she had freshmen compositions to read, thick piles of them, the first batch of the new semester. As the least senior member of the English department, she had a heavy schedule of the required freshman courses, with one notable exception: the twentieth-century novel. She didn't mind trying to inflict writing standards on future paper technologists and environmental experts, but it was sheer joy to spend three class periods a week with students who'd willingly elected to study the contemporary novel.

Three of the first seven papers she read had incomplete sentences; one had eighteen misspelled words, and two had little to do with the assignment and seemed suspiciously similar to papers she'd read during the first semester of the course. Didn't she deserve a few minutes of recreational reading before she plowed through more themes?

The book had cost $14.95, but with the dust jacket ripped, it wasn't even a good collectible first edition. She might as well get some reading pleasure from it. If the story line was as depressing as she feared, Adam's novel would be easy to put aside. A half hour was all she could spare this evening.

Reading Adam Smith-Woodham was nothing like talking to him. In person he was soft-spoken, casual in his use of words, never trying to impress anyone with the depth of his scholarship or his command of the language. Hester let herself remember some of their conversations, relieved that the initial shock of seeing his book had worn off. She'd never forget him, of course, but no one stayed in love after nearly three years of separation, especially not when their situation had been so hopeless from the beginning. Adam had been unhappy, hurt by his wife's neglect as she pursued her own career as a dancer, and Hester met him as an adoring graduate student, awed by his success, flattered that a widely heralded author nearly seven years her senior was interested in spending time with her.

A half hour passed as she read, and then an hour; Hester forgot about freshman compositions and the classes she had to teach in the morning. Adam caught her up in his story, almost against her will, until she was incapable of putting the book aside.

The Farewell Rock was their story. Adam had changed their physical appearances, but nothing external could disguise the identities of the main characters. The hero was the author, devastated by the widening gulf between himself and his wife and enchanted by a young student. The heroine had wispy blond hair and blue eyes instead of Hester's thick, coppery-red mane and changeable hazel eyes, but little else about the "other woman" was different.

Adam had used her in his book! At first mildly flattered, she read with increasing intensity and misgivings, plowing into the complexities of the story with growing disbelief.

14

Practically every scene with the young woman, Jenny, had actually happened!

The detailed account of their first meeting was exactly as she remembered it. When his first session as a guest lecturer had been over, she'd summoned all her courage to ask him to autograph three of his books: paperbacks, not first editions, unfortunately all she could afford on her work-study grant. He'd been wonderfully congenial, asking her to have coffee at the local doughnut shop, putting her completely at ease. Being with him felt so comfortable! Barely six feet tall himself, he insisted that he loved tall women, making her see her five foot ten height as an asset, not a liability, convincing her that he sincerely appreciated everything about her.

We belonged together, she thought miserably, the pain of separation coming back with each page she read.

When they met, the New England winter was at its fierce peak, driving them to meet in warm public places. In the early spring he took her to his cottage, the windows still boarded against the battering of Atlantic gales. There, by the real Farewell Rock, they'd faced the truth: their love had no place to go. Adam was still tied to his wife by the bonds of the past and wanted time to work out his situation. Hester, young and perhaps impatient, hurt because he couldn't make the total commitment she needed, issued an ultimatum. She didn't want to be the other woman in his life. That was the last time she saw him.

Acting as the catalyst that brought the plot to the crisis point, her part in his new book was crucial. Only the ache in her eyes and the raw feeling in her heart finally made her put the book aside. With another hundred pages to read, she had very little of the night left for sleep. Falling into bed, she felt as if she'd just closed her eyes when the insistent beeping of her alarm woke her to face another day of classes.

In the morning Adam's book seemed like a grim joke—on her. Were all his novels based so faithfully on his own experiences? If so, she'd been a prize fool for thinking she meant something special to him. His books were big on affairs; maybe she'd only been one of many love interests in his life.

Her aging blue compact car wouldn't start on this subzero morning, and missing a class was a very bad idea for an instructor who was being considered for tenure that spring. Did Russ Michaels have an early class? The assistant basketball coach also taught physical education and might have to be on campus early. Reluctantly she knocked on the door of his second-floor apartment right above hers, relieved that he answered in his work clothes, which for Russ meant red knit sweat pants and shirt with the school emblem.

"Do you have a class this morning, Russ?" she asked, pulling off her driving gloves and rubbing her fingers to restore circulation. "My car is frozen solid, I guess."

"Glad to run you up." Russ smiled down on her from his six and a half feet, showing her he was delighted.

Her undergraduate social life had been dominated by basketball players who looked at her height and striking good looks and had visions of seven-foot sons on the all-American list. There weren't many eligible bachelors on Halsted's campus, but she tried not to encourage her neighbor. He was good-natured and nice-looking with dark hair and blue eyes, but raising her own basketball team wasn't in Hester's plans for the future.

"You look beat," Russ said sympathetically after his gasguzzling Buick, old enough to be comfortably roomy for his long legs, coughed into action.

"I had a late night correcting papers."

This wasn't a total falsehood; she certainly wished she'd corrected more of them instead of tormenting herself with Adam's version of their brief love.

"Coming to the game tonight?" Russ asked.

"Here?"

"Yes, against Beloit."

"Oh, of course." She'd forgotten about the big game of the season, not the best way to stay in favor with the assistant coach. "Not tonight, I'm afraid. I'm swamped with work."

"I don't know why every college requires English," he said, not sounding as funny as he thought he was. "Nearly made me ineligible my first year."

She was grateful for the ride, so she didn't suggest that

16

some people couldn't care less which team had the best basketball players.

Halsted College was privately endowed, funded mostly by alumni and the industry that benefited from the paper technology program, a specialty of the school. Like most small collegiate institutions with an enrollment of under a thousand, Halsted had to scramble for students, dollars, and competent instructors, finding it impossible to match the varied programs or the higher salaries offered by state universities. Before meeting Adam, Hester had never considered going to a small liberal arts school in the Midwest; armed with several years' teaching experience at a junior college and an MA in English literature, she'd been hoping to find a place in a college on the Eastern Seaboard. Adam had changed her plans.

Like her namesake, Hester in *The Scarlet Letter,* she saw the wilderness as a refuge, never mind that she was far from the timbered wilds of northern Wisconsin. At first, while she finished her degree and searched for a job, she and Adam had corresponded, sending feverish, longing letters that solved nothing. She'd burned her bridges and his letters, taking care not to leave a forwarding address where he could discover it, when the job offer came from Halsted. Only her family in Norfolk, Maine, knew where she was. Adam had written to her there, but her mother sent his letters back, writing *Address Unknown* on the envelopes. She didn't approve of the deception until Hester told her the letters came from a married man.

Hester absolutely did not have time to finish Adam's book that evening. After classes were over for the day, there was a long interdepartmental meeting to discuss the closing of a building built in 1892. The one glaring disadvantage in teaching at a venerable old institution was that the campus had more than its share of drafty, deteriorating white elephants. All that held together the old social sciences building was the ivy, and the maintenance department insisted that the thick foliage had wormed its tendrils into the crumbling mortar between the bricks and caused damage too costly to repair. The history department was understandably

17

disturbed about the prospect of teaching in janitors' closets and crawl spaces. The English department was sympathetic but protective of its own space.

After a long, indecisive meeting, Hester had dinner with Constance Hardin, a young, lively, sophisticated black woman in her mid-thirties who was head of the speech and drama department. They frequently got together for meals, concerts, lectures, or the theater when their busy schedules allowed it.

"Oh, before I forget, I brought a lecture notice for you," Constance said over a dinner of Lake Superior whitefish in one of the town's few restaurants that didn't specialize in beer and pizza.

As a graduate of the University of Wisconsin, Constance was still in touch with all the activities on the big campus. Occasionally, in good weather, the two of them would attend an event there, but it did mean a drive of over a hundred miles one way.

"I thought you might be interested in this Adam Smith-Woodham lecture," Constance went on. "Aren't you teaching a course on the twentieth-century novel this semester?"

"Yes," Hester said woodenly, wondering if this was how it felt to be haunted. As hard as she'd tried to put the man out of her mind, he just wouldn't stay buried in the past. "But I don't think I can go."

"Well, keep the information in case you change your mind. I'm tied up with rehearsals for the Madrigal Dinner every night this week, but maybe someone in your department would be interested."

"Thanks." Hester stuffed the paper into her purse only because she didn't want to hurt her friend's feelings by ripping it up.

Later at home she wondered if it was fair to read students' work in the evening when she was totally exhausted. She decided to get up early instead and tackle them before her first class, which fortunately didn't meet until 10:00 A.M. on Thursdays. After nearly dozing off in a hot tub scented with bath oil, she felt relaxed enough to sleep around the clock.

That was before she let herself think about *The Farewell Rock*. After a half hour of restless wakefulness, she gave up. Adam's book demanded to be finished. She had to know how he felt about their final parting.

The lovers were standing by the rock, the sand still hard underfoot from the winter freeze. The heroine, Jenny, was wearing an emerald-green windbreaker just like the one Hester had actually worn that day. As he got closer to the end of the book, Adam was even less concerned with disguising his characters. Jenny's hair was whipping around her face, and Daniel caught a tendril between his thumb and finger, pressing it to his cheek, a gesture that was painfully familiar to Hester.

> "Take this, at least," he said, trying to hand her the box with the opal pendant.
> "I've always believed opals are bad luck." She was trying hard not to cry, staring at the milky stone he dangled to let the wintry sun catch the streaks of fire in its depths.
> "Our luck will change."
> "There isn't any luck left for the two of us."

Hester remembered these words so well that tears streamed down her face, the old wounds torn open. Every sentence hurt, but she could no more put the book down than she could forget Adam.

> He led her into the cottage, kicking the door shut and taking her in his arms. . . .

That wasn't at all the way their story ended! Outrage was a mild emotion compared to what she felt as the fictional man and woman slowly and sensuously shed their garments in the glowing orange light from the rough stone fireplace.

> Her breasts were small but perfect, with dark, womanly nipples. . . .

19

Hester's face was feverish as Adam's imagination consummated the union of Daniel and Jenny. Was this his revenge because Hester had disappeared from his life? She felt stripped and branded by the intimately personal details swimming on the page in front of her. He was such a skillful writer! How could he use his talent to make a mockery of the very special feelings that had existed between them? His heroine was wildly passionate in a love scene that went on and on and on, until Hester wanted to scream at the author to stop it. Leave something private! The scene was every man's fantasy of total physical love, but it wasn't what they'd experienced in real life!

Hester had read about the hero's groping attempts to rekindle his wife's love without disapproving; she was a tolerant reader, willing to sample the strongest kinds of literature if the writing was excellent. This scene was different! Knowing that Adam was describing what he wished had happened between them left her devastated.

Would the characters in his book live happily ever after? She read mechanically after the shattering love scene, not really caring about the ending now that she felt so exposed and exploited. He'd even described her bottom as "boyish, except when she padded naked across the floor, the cheeks wiggling provocatively." How could he! He made her feel like a cocktail waitress wearing skin-tight leotards and a furry tail to call attention to her rump!

The lines of print went through her mind like material fed into a computer, each word stored in her bank of rage, until the last chapter when the couple parted. Impassioned lovemaking wasn't enough to sustain their relationship without total commitment. Hester had always known it wouldn't be enough for her, but refusing Adam had been punishing self-denial. Even before reading his book, she only needed to imagine him beside her in bed, holding and touching her, to suffer from "midnight longing."

How could he be so unfair? It didn't matter if no other person ever knew that the young woman in *The Farewell Rock* was alive and well and teaching freshman English at Halsted College. She knew!

Slamming the cover shut on the final sentence, she threw the book across the bedroom, hearing a cracking noise from the binding. For the first time in her nearly twenty-nine years, she'd abused a book, but she felt more damaged herself than the volume was.

Crawling out of bed, she went to the makeshift bookshelves in her living room, assembled from concrete blocks and planks she'd painted a dark green. All of Adam's books were there, the three autographed paperbacks, her prized first edition of his first published novel, a treasure plucked at a charity booksale for a dollar, and a copy of his second book, the first to win critical acclaim. *The Farewell Rock* was a departure from the others, a love story, although there was a hefty dose of sex in all his books. How many scenes in the others were real, taken from Adam's experiences, stolen from women who really cared about him? It was just as well she'd never know.

She didn't reread the lecture notice stuck in a deep corner of her large leather shoulder bag until Saturday morning when she was waiting in line to pay for groceries. Wouldn't she like to tell Adam Smith-Woodham what she thought of his book! Even his hyphenated name irritated her, never mind that his enlightened mother had insisted on adding her name, Woodham, to her husband's Smith. Maybe the gentle, loving man she remembered was really a pretentious bore and a womanizer. Adam was lucky that publicity would be poison to her career and terrible for her nerves, or he might have a lawsuit on his hands. How could an author "borrow" someone else's most personal feelings and squeeze a sexy story from them? She hated him. Yes, she really did hate the author of *The Farewell Rock*.

Except for Miss Richardson, who was semiretired and taught only one poetry course each semester, Hester was the sole woman and the only single person in the English department. Her associates, including Professor Solaski, the department head, had all risen above the lowly rank of instructor and occasionally lorded it over her, but generally they were a congenial group, cooperative on the rare occasions when she needed help steering a safe course through the politics of academic life. But when it came to accompanying her to a lecture at the university, they were useless. Not even Bob Solaski's chubby, good-hearted wife was understanding enough to send him off to Madison if Hester asked him.

Not sure if it was curiosity or sheer craziness, Hester knew she had to hear Adam's lecture Wednesday night. He was touring to promote his book, of course, but what was he saying about it? Would he hint to his audiences, largely female, no doubt, that *The Farewell Rock* was a story drawn heavily from his own experiences? She was probably being melodramatic, expecting some startling revelation from his lecture, but thinking about Adam and his book was robbing her of sleep and ruining her concentration.

On Tuesday she went through the faculty directory, trying to think of someone who would enjoy the lecture enough to ride to Madison with her. Constance was busy and so were friends in the music and political science departments. She tried a few faculty wives, including Mrs. Solaski, but basketball was king this year. Some of the most unlikely people had become fans since the team's recent spectacular victories, and Wednesday night there was another big home game.

Hester was an only child who'd grown up in a very small town; she'd learned early not to miss out on things she wanted to do for lack of a companion. Her last class ended at three on Wednesday, and by three ten she was in her car heading southwest, watching with a tinge of anxiety as the windshield wipers pushed aside powdery particles of snow. Much to her relief the flurries subsided a few miles out of town, and the road was dry and ice-free, thanks to the state's efficient highway crews. Adam's lecture started at seven, so with a little luck she'd start for home by nine. She tried to convince herself that the weather was the source of her uneasiness, but the hardhearted Yankee in her wouldn't buy it.

The lecture was being held at the Memorial Union, hopefully in a large room where she wouldn't be noticed by the speaker. Her heavy coils of red hair were pinned up and hidden under an awful fur hat, a Christmas gift from her Aunt Lucinda years ago. It made her look like a Cossack in the czar's palace guard, adding about four unwanted inches to her height. She was planning to wear her reading glasses, prescribed for tired graduate-student eyes but rarely used, and to get there early enough to find a seat in the farthest, darkest corner. Adam never arrived early for a lecture; he liked to wait until the crowd settled down, although he was generous with his time afterward, always staying for questions, introductions, and autographs. His natural ease with people was one of the things she loved—had loved—about him. As an English teacher, she'd better remember to keep everything about Adam in the past tense.

Turning up the volume on the car radio, she hummed along with some obnoxiously loud hard rock that she ordinarily detested, trying to drown out the turmoil that threatened to boil over and shatter her composure. One thing she did not want was an emotional confrontation with Adam Smith-Woodham. She had her feelings wrapped up in a very tidy package, no thanks to the famous author, and this trip was intended only to satisfy her curiosity. Anyone in her situation would want to hear what the novelist had to say for himself.

Hester, Hester, he be a married man.

She was imagining a whole row of miniature Puritan women lined up on her dashboard, shaking bonneted heads at their foolhardy descendant. Well, this time she didn't need her ancestors' warnings to remind her that Adam could only bring her heartache. After hearing what he had to say about *The Farewell Rock,* she'd put him out of her mind for good and forever.

Approaching Madison on I-94, she had to switch on the windshield wipers again. She was used to rugged Maine winters; there was nothing alarming about a little snow. With a bit of luck she'd drive out of it when she headed east toward Lake Michigan to go home.

23

CHAPTER TWO

The room was large but crowded, all the folding chairs occupied ten minutes before Adam's lecture was scheduled to begin. From her seat in the last row, Hester overheard more than one group of women decide to stay, even though it meant standing. The podium looked starkly academic against a backdrop of heavy drapes, but the room seemed to buzz with anticipation. Her survey of the crowd convinced her that this was a rarity on the college lecture circuit: a full house without compulsory student attendance. Adam Smith-Woodham was a big drawing card, but then, he always had been.

He walked into the room smiling with confidence, then inclined his head attentively, listening to the professor chosen to do the introduction. In a camel's-hair jacket with leather elbow patches, Adam looked very much like a professor himself, but his dark brown slacks and sweater vest, worn with a white shirt open at his neck, reminded Hester of his flair for casual elegance. He rarely wore neckties and hated formal wear, but still managed to be the most striking man present in most situations. His straight sandy hair was trimmed shorter than it was in the book-cover photo, but it was still thick, setting off rugged, uneven features and sensuously firm lips. Only his eyes were outstanding, deep-set and amber-brown, but intelligence and a lively interest in people gave him appeal and charm. He'd shaved his beard, revealing a strong, square chin with just a hint of a cleft. His face was likable, even trustworthy, but physical characteristics didn't explain his magnetism.

Hester dug her nails into her palms, willing away the attraction she'd unconsciously felt when he entered the room. Nothing he could say or do would rekindle what she'd once felt for him. She was determined to hear his presentation, then put him out of her mind permanently. All she needed to know was whether he was publicizing his novel as autobiographical.

"Good evening." His voice, deep and commanding, flowed over an absolutely still crowd.

He had the gift of speaking to a large group in such a way that each listener felt personally addressed.

Hester was warm in her heavy fur hat and pile-lined leather boots, and the reading glasses were an irritation, perched on the end of her nose so she could see over them. Wearing a bulky white cotton-knit sweater under her brown tweed suit had been a good idea on Halsted's energy-conscious campus, but here the thermostat seemed to be set at ninety. She eased out of her suit jacket, trying not to attract attention. Adam had excellent vision, and he liked eye contact with individuals in the audience. Unfortunately the girl in front of her was scarcely five feet tall and provided no shield.

It was difficult to remember Adam was there to sell his book. He was a witty entertainer, drawing on many sources to relate amusing anecdotes. His topic was an intriguing one: Romantic Love as Seen by Male Authors. His conclusion was that men could be as romantic as women when they listened to their instincts. He didn't leave many unbelievers, but Hester was one of them. In his book he'd turned their romance into a romp in the hay; she wasn't going to forgive or forget that, not ever!

The audience applauded enthusiastically when his prepared talk was over, but no one left the room. Instead they responded to his invitation to stay and chat awhile. Hester wanted to disappear, but she needed a milling crowd to leave

25

unseen. Adam fielded a number of questions, humorously evasive about his personal life but honest and helpful when asked about his working habits and professional background. The crowd was in the palm of his hand, Hester realized, but she didn't want to be there with them, not this time.

Working the sleeves of her jacket over the thick arms of the sweater without standing was an awkward maneuver, but she didn't want to tower conspicuously over the people seated around her. There was no real reason to feel so much urgency about leaving; if the snow had continued to fall, delaying was to her advantage. It would give the plows time to clear the highways. She wasn't afraid that Adam would see her and catch up; there was a good chance he was too hurt by her disappearance to care about seeing her again. Hester had wiggled into her forest-green coat and was waiting for her row to file out when she realized Adam had changed his routine. Instead of staying to visit after the question period, he'd disappeared from the front of the room.

Beside her a snowy-haired couple, two little dumpling people who were wearing enough winter clothing to stock a secondhand shop, finally moved out of the way, allowing Hester to bolt toward the exit. Even with the delay, she might have escaped if her reflexes hadn't betrayed her. She turned automatically when she heard her name, forgetting that only one person in the room knew it.

"Hester, wait!"

She was being swept along by the crowd, but not quickly enough. Adam was only a few feet away when she decided to run, and then it was too late.

"Hester, I can't believe it's you!"

He took her arm, steering her toward the door and keeping a firm hold.

"It is." She wanted to sound sullen and betrayed, but her husky, melodic voice betrayed her. She only sounded stunned.

"Where can we go? Let me collect my coat and get out of here. Hessie, where have you been?"

His words spilled out, confused and harsh and excited.

"Adam, I have to leave. . . ."

"Not without me! My coat's down this way."

He half dragged her to a small office, retrieved his coat before a grateful professor could do more than stammer a quick "Thanks for coming," and carried it outside the Union, not willing to release her long enough to don it.

"You'll freeze," she said.

"Better that than let you disappear again. Where the bloody hell have you been? My letters came back, your family wouldn't tell me—"

"Will you please let go of me and put on your coat?"

"I will, but don't move, not one step. I can still outrun you."

He'd proven that once on a dark, snowy night when the campus was deserted, racing her to a statue of the founder, making her forfeit a kiss when she lost. That scene had been in his book too!

"I really have to—"

"Stay!"

He slipped into the storm coat, tying it below the thick fur collar, stuffing one gloveless hand in a pocket and coiling the other around her arm.

"So," he said, catching his breath with a heavy sigh, "this is where you've been hiding."

"No, I just came for the lecture." She immediately regretted saying that.

"From where?"

"Does it really matter, Adam?"

"To me it does," he said grimly. "Are you teaching?"

"Yes."

"Near here?"

"Not so near."

"I like to play Twenty Questions. Do you work at a college within fifty miles?"

They were walking rapidly, but not in the direction of her car.

"No."

"It doesn't matter whether you tell me. I'll just follow you home. You're not going to disappear on me again."

"Adam!" She stopped abruptly; wearing high-heeled boots put her eyes level with his. "Adam," she repeated softly, not knowing what to say.

"Do you have a car?" he asked more gently.

"Yes."

"We'll come back for it later. I'm in a VIP parking spot back near the Union."

"It's snowing. I have a long drive."

"You can't drive in this."

"The highways back to Vienne get good attention." She realized what she'd said, but if he heard, he didn't comment.

Adam led her to a burgundy Chrysler New Yorker that looked nearly black as heavy snow dimmed the nearby light. With a feeling of unreality she got in when he opened the door, wondering miserably if he'd use this good-bye scene in a future book. Since reading *The Farewell Rock,* she'd thought of a hundred scathing things to say to him, but now only her hurt slipped out.

"You used me in your book."

"Used you?" He was sitting behind the wheel, but the door was still open, allowing him to look at her under the brightness of the dome light. "What happened between us meant a great deal to me!"

"You think it didn't to me?"

"Take off that hat."

"What?"

"That's the most ridiculous hat I've ever seen." He never wore hats himself.

She reached up and touched it, toppling it to one side at a silly angle. Rather than look like a fool, she pulled it off, feeling her upswept hair tumble down, spilling heavy coppery waves to her shoulders.

"My aunt would be crushed if she heard you say that." She laughed weakly, a nervous little outburst that somehow made him the winner of round one.

"When did you start wearing glasses?" he asked softly.

"I don't. . . ." Darn, she never had been a good liar. "Not all the time."

"This is a disguise, then?"

He reached out and pulled them off her nose. She'd steeled herself for angry accusations and new pain, but not for the gentle, seeking kiss that he pressed on her lips.

"Hessie." Only he called her that; her family weren't ones to bestow nicknames.

"Adam, I don't think—"

She couldn't think, not with his lips caressing her eyelids, his breath warm on her forehead, his hand sliding under the coils of hair at the back of her neck.

"I thought I'd go crazy when you dropped out of sight," he said softly, kissing her with a sweetness that almost made her forget his betrayal.

"Your book," she said turning her head.

"Did you like it?"

"It was well written, the characterizations were strong . . . I hated it!"

"Hated it?" He didn't sound as if he believed her.

"Everything we did, everything we felt, you used it all."

"Because it was so important to me."

"But the end of our story was nothing like the book!"

"The end of our story hasn't been written yet, not since I've found you again."

"You haven't found me!" She tried to shrug his arm from her shoulder, but he wasn't having it.

"Technically I guess you found me. I'm very glad you came tonight, Hessie."

"I only came to find out if you'd tell people the book was an autobiography."

"No, I haven't. But can you condemn me for using my fondest fantasies along with my deepest feelings?"

"You made our private feelings public!"

"Is that what you really object to?" He finally closed the door, switching on the dome light manually and taking her face between two cold, gloveless hands.

"That, and the things that never happened," she insisted.

29

"Some situations aren't as complicated in books as they are in real life."

"You mean a few torrid scenes never hurt your sales."

"If that's a verbal slap in the face, I accept it. But you're wrong, Hessie. What we had was beautiful; the unbelievable part is that we were together so much and never made love."

"Your wife—"

"Came between us, yes. I'm divorced now, Hessie."

"Congratulations." She didn't hold back her pain.

"Do you want me to say I never should've loved you?" he asked.

"I don't want you to say anything!" She opened the door but his hand restrained her.

"We need to talk."

"No, Adam. Please, no."

"You can't drive home in this storm. Let me help you find a motel room, then we'll have some dinner. I haven't had a bite since noon."

He never ate before a big lecture, she remembered. In spite of his calm, poised exterior, he got a little jittery before speaking to large groups, preferring to perform on an empty stomach.

Wrenching free, she stepped out into what was now a howling gale. The snow was blowing furiously, and it didn't take much imagination to anticipate blocked roads and hazardous traveling conditions.

"At least let me drive you to your car," Adam said from inside his car.

"It is bad," she admitted reluctantly, slipping back into the vehicle.

"I'll lead you to the motel where I'm staying. If you can't get a room there, at least let me see you settled somewhere else. I wouldn't drive to Vienne tonight myself."

He'd remembered the name of the town. She didn't know how she felt about that.

Following his car, she could barely see the red taillights ten feet ahead. The decision to stay overnight was out of her hands. No sane person would risk the highways tonight except in a dire emergency, but when she thought of how it felt

30

to be kissed again by Adam, she wavered. Maybe the storm outside was less hazardous than the one inside her mind.

Snowflakes melted on her hair and dripped to her forehead, and the shoulders of her coat were damp after she walked through the blizzardy parking area to the registration desk. Thank heavens there was a room available! She wouldn't feel safe until a door with a night bolt and a chain stood between Adam and her.

The motel restaurant was closed, but the lounge was cozy and inviting, providing a sandwich selection for late-evening snacking.

The last thing Hester wanted was food, but she let herself be swept along by Adam's determination, fatalistically deciding a confrontation had to take place sometime. Wouldn't it be better to let him know right now that his book had destroyed the last of her romantic illusions about him?

Low round tables and leather-padded chairs were scattered at random, movable to accommodate small parties or large groups. A deserted platform held a sign announcing the vocalist who would be entertaining there on the weekend, but tonight there was no music. Except for a few scattered couples and some men at the bar, they were the only customers. Adam led the way to a dark corner secluded by a large rubber plant in a room divider.

"What would you like?" he asked after the waitress, costumed in western garb with a flirtatiously short skirt, left sandwich lists with them.

"Nothing. Well, maybe some wine."

"Chablis?" he asked.

"You do remember little details," she said uncomfortably.

"About you, I do."

"That was obvious in your book."

"Hester, I never thought you'd react this way. In fact . . ." He stopped and pretended to read the menu.

"In fact what?" She hated unfinished sentences!

"You'll be angry."

"I am angry, Adam."

"I didn't expect you to be. I thought you'd read my new book and . . ."

31

A hesitant Adam, breaking off his thoughts, groping for words, was a man she didn't know. But then, had she ever really known the person behind the sophisticated author and lecturer?

"I did read it," she said dryly.

"I know. And it brought you to hear me."

"Yes," she admitted reluctantly, "but only because I didn't appreciate what you wrote. I needed to know what you were saying to promote the book."

"As you heard, very little."

"Why?"

He shrugged his shoulders. "It's one thing to write about things that mean a great deal to me and another to spill my guts in a public lecture."

"The harm has already been done in the book." She felt terribly weary.

"Harm!" He seemed about to explode, but the waitress returned for their order.

"She'll have a glass of Chablis, and I'll have the club sandwich with coffee."

"How could you believe I'd be thrilled about having our whole friendship documented in a novel?" Hester asked when they were alone again.

"Friendship! Documented! Hester, you sound like a throwback to your puritanical ancestors. We were in love!"

"I'm proud of my heritage," she said stiffly, too shaken by his vehemence to talk about love.

"I was in love anyway," he said unhappily. "Even authors have their groupies, I guess."

"If you think I was only impressed with your name on the *New York Times* best-seller list . . ."

"You wouldn't be the first graduate student to have a crush on a visiting lecturer."

"This is too much." She stood so abruptly the chair thudded into the wainscoting behind it. "Good-bye, Adam."

Her long stride carried her through the lobby and into a corridor that led to the sleeping units, but she was too upset to remember her room number. After digging for the key she'd dropped into her deep coat pocket, she forced herself to slow her retreat long enough to read the tag: room 242. Somewhere there had to be stairs to the second floor. The hallways, carpeted in rusty orange with pale green walls, seemed like a maze, and her sense of direction failed her as her eyes blurred, a condition she blamed on the wretched glasses she'd worn during the lecture. A mature college instructor didn't blubber over a burnt-out love affair! More by chance than otherwise, she found the stairs and her room, banging the door behind her and jamming the bolt in place.

How could he doubt that she'd loved him? For three deliriously happy months she'd tried to deceive herself into believing Adam would leave his wife for her. Talk about school girl naïveté!

"He's divorced now," a little voice hissed in Hester's head, but she wasn't buying it. For all she knew, Adam's wife had left him. Maybe she'd gotten disgusted with his roving eye; maybe she'd hated having their personal life documented in his novels. Yes, documented! It was a perfectly accurate word for what Adam had done, writing about the tiniest details of their relationship. He'd even described the way her tongue slipped between her lips when she concentrated!

Her first impulse was to go home, storm or no storm, but a glance out the window squelched that idea. Below in the parking area, cars were shrouded in several inches of snow, and the driving wind was piling up drifts that would make leaving the motel nearly impossible. She shivered, thinking of how comforting her favorite red flannel nightgown would feel, then remembered that what she was wearing was what she had to wear.

At least she could take a warm shower, which she did, drying off briskly and putting on her slip, the only part of her outfit comfortable enough for sleeping. She wished for a toothbrush but swirled water in her mouth rather than hunt for a vending machine that sold one and risk seeing Adam in the corridor.

Flicking on the TV, which she rarely had time to watch, she crawled under the covers in one of the room's two large double beds.

The knock on her door didn't surprise her, but she ignored it at first, still too agitated to see more of Adam. His pounding was softly civilized but maddeningly persistent. He wasn't going to be discouraged easily. If she had sleeping neighbors, they'd be justified in complaining to the management.

There was more to be said between them, and she was too keyed up to hope for sleep that night unless their break was final and irreversible. Gathering an olive-green blanket around her shoulders like an oversize shawl, she covered herself and opened the door.

"You weren't sleeping." It was an accusation, not a question.

"I was trying to." Don't give an inch, she warned herself sternly.

"May I come in?"

"Only for a few minutes."

"If that's what you want."

"It is. Definitely." Did that firm, positive voice come from her?

Still carrying his coat in the crook of his arm, he closed the door.

"Can we start over?" he asked.

"What do you mean?"

"Pretend we've just now met again."

"I don't want to play games, Adam."

"Indulge me. I'll leave sooner if you do."

"All right. Start over." She retreated and sat on the end of the bed, making a secure cocoon from neck to toes out of the blanket.

"Hessie, how wonderful to see you. Where've you been all this time?"

"Hello, Adam. I've been teaching."

"Oh, where?"

"Halsted College. In the English department." He knew the city; there was no point in being coy about the school.

"Do you enjoy your work?" He laid his coat on a chair and sat beside her.

"Very much, thank you."

34

"Don't you want to ask what I've been doing?"

"I already know: writing *The Farewell Rock.*"

"And have you had a chance to read my new book?"

"For pity's sake, Adam! You already know I have!"

"How could I know that if we've just met this minute?"

"We haven't!"

"But we're starting over, remember?"

"Only so you'll leave sooner!"

"Agreed. And how did you like my novel?"

"It was excellent, as usual. Well written, maybe even brilliant, I don't know."

"Of course you know! Your business is literary criticism. Isn't that what you teach your students?"

"Stop, Adam!"

"I'm not mocking you, Hessie."

"Aren't you?" She stood and walked to the window, covered now by heavy insulated drapes, parting them to stare out at the wind-whipped whiteness below.

"No, I'm trying to understand why you cut me off without even a note of good-bye." He followed her to the window.

"There wasn't any future for us." She pulled the blanket more tightly around her shoulders, aware of his closeness and weakened by it.

"You couldn't be sure of that."

"Did you leave your wife?"

He rested one hand on her shoulder and hesitated for a long moment. "She left me."

"I appreciate your honesty."

"I've never lied to you about anything, Hessie."

The misery in his voice was enough to make her face him, wanting to offer some kind of comfort but restrained by her own inner turmoil.

"No, maybe not," she said softly.

"The marriage was over before I met you. I didn't want it to end, but loving you made me realize that I could go on without Joanna."

"At the beach." Her breath was hurting her chest. "That's not what you told me there."

35

"No, my feelings hadn't yet crystallized. I needed time. I'm deeply sorry that you couldn't give it to me."

"Don't try to make me feel guilty, Adam."

"I'm trying to make me not feel guilty."

"Is that sentence grammatical?" She looked away.

Don't watch television in the dark, her mother always warned. If she'd listened, she wouldn't be standing in a dark room with only the warm glow of a small color set washing over the man beside her, making him look mystical and commanding, like a mythical king gathering his warriors around a campfire.

She did nothing except tilt her chin just a bit; with bare feet she was a little shorter than Adam.

His lips felt wonderful, warm and firm, moving over hers with gentle seductiveness. Strong, lean fingers pushed back her hair, enjoying the silky thickness. Reaching for his shoulders, she let go of the blanket, feeling the rush of cool air as the covering bunched around her ankles.

No one kissed like Adam; his mouth issued an invitation and dared her to respond. She was the first to press her tongue beyond the barrier of strong, square teeth, forgetting as she did so everything but the man and the moment. Her lonely midnight longings rose up to engulf her now, putting her within reach of the only fulfillment she'd ever dreamed about.

Adam let his jacket drop to the floor, but she scarcely noticed. The nylon of her slip heightened every sensation on the bare skin underneath, and his hands moving up and down her back were driving her crazy with desire. It was a form of temporary insanity to desperately want the man who had hurt her so much.

"I've missed you, Hessie. I don't have words to tell you how much."

He lifted her, making her feel dainty and petite for the first time in her life, slowly carrying her to the bed, where the blankets were turned down for her solitary use.

Leaning over her, Adam looked deeply into her eyes, dark greenish-gray in the dim light, and sighed heavily before kissing her again with heart-stopping thoroughness.

She felt vulnerable to her core, more naked than the absence of clothing could ever make her feel. She'd made a terrible mistake years ago in loving a married man. Now he was free, but that didn't erase the memory of the months of agony she'd spent waiting for him to come to her. One thing hadn't changed: she still wanted to be in his arms. Could she let herself respond to him, knowing she risked being hurt again? Divorce had left a void in his life, but she didn't want to be a temporary fill-in.

"No," she barely managed to whisper.

She'd been living with a memory, a ghost of happiness past, but it wasn't spectral love that caused her racing pulse and pounding heart.

"No," he repeated, but he didn't stop kissing her, moving his lips over the smooth column of her neck.

His hands were warm on her shoulders, fingering the narrow straps of her slip. So tense, she was trembling, she reached toward him, burying her fingers in the hair above his collar.

"Hessie, I missed you so much. When we said good-bye at the beach—"

"At *The Farewell Rock!*" Remembering the scene in his book made her freeze in his arms and avert her face from his eyes.

"I invented that name," he said, sounding puzzled.

"Like you invented the end of the book!" She squirmed free and moved away.

"We have a lot to talk about," he said quietly.

"Please, just go, Adam."

She found the discarded blanket and wrapped it around herself.

"Go, just like that? After looking for you all this time? No." He shook his head.

"There's nothing to talk about," she insisted, still avoiding his eyes.

"There's everything to talk about! We have years to catch up on. Not a single day has passed that I haven't wished you were with me."

"Now you're exaggerating!"

She desperately wanted to believe him, but the past made it impossible.

"Sit down. Please." He gestured toward the bed.

Shaking her head, she adjusted the blanket more securely around her shoulders.

"Then stand." He shrugged dejectedly and moved several steps closer.

The hurt on his face wasn't easy to endure, but she backed away again, focusing her gaze on a little thread matted on the carpet.

"Hessie . . ."

"I really wish you'd leave, Adam."

"If that's the way you feel . . ."

"It is."

"Maybe it would be best for now." He moved stiffly toward his jacket on the floor and put it on. "I'll go if you promise to meet me for breakfast. Please, Hessie."

The little strangled sound she made could've meant yes, no, or nothing at all.

"Is seven too early?" he asked. "I'll meet you in the restaurant downstairs."

Taking her silence for assent, he quietly left.

She didn't sleep; it never occurred to her that she would. In one short night she relived every moment with Adam, past and present, shaken to the core by her overwhelming reaction to him. At first she felt humiliated for responding so quickly to his kisses and was afraid she'd never regain her self-respect. Gradually, as the night passed and she lay in open-eyed misery, she stopped worrying about having made a fool of herself. Adam wouldn't see her reaction to him in that way, and she shouldn't either. She knew Adam was still attracted to her, but she had to consider the past instead of fretting about one impassioned, impulsive moment of weakness.

Maybe she still loved Adam, but it was too late for a fresh beginning. There'd always be *The Farewell Rock* and his broken promise: he hadn't gone back to his wife to make the final break. Hester had waited in vain while he avoided making a decision. She had lacked patience then, but with good

38

reason: no woman wanted to wait on the sidelines while a man decided whether his marriage was on or off.

Adam was a man who thrived on companionship and close relationships. His life probably seemed empty without a wife, but Hester didn't want to be the woman who caught him on the rebound because he was lonely. Seeing him again didn't change the fact that he hadn't chosen to come to her. Instead he'd tried to work things out with his wife. His lack of decisiveness had told all she needed to know: She wasn't the most important person in his life. Nothing he could say or do now would change the past, and seeing more of him would only cause heartbreak.

Dressing before dawn, she looked down on the parking area with misgivings. It wasn't quite five thirty and no plows had shoveled aside the drifts. Hurriedly checking out, she struggled through drifts that topped her boots, finding the snowy mound that was her car. At least here luck was with her: the wind had swept clear the drive behind her compact, and it looked as if she'd be able to get to the street, already plowed by a city crew laboring through the night.

Brushing off the snow was a big job, but she felt rewarded when her car rammed through the last hurdle—the snow pushed across the exit by the plow—and gained access to the street.

She rallied all her considerable courage for the trip home on snow-scoured roads, some with only one lane open to vehicles. Driving was hazardous enough to keep her mind occupied. For a while she pushed aside thoughts of her cowardice: leaving without talking to Adam. The raw elements in a bad Wisconsin winter storm weren't nearly as threatening as coming face-to-face with him again.

Exhausted but temporarily triumphant, she arrived at her first class on time.

CHAPTER THREE

"Hester, what size dress do you wear?" Constance's voice on the phone sounded mischievous.

"Why do you want to know?" Hester glanced at her officemate, Brad Harris, but he was absorbed in an article he was hoping to publish in a professional journal.

"I have a very good reason." Constance couldn't suppress a throaty giggle.

"Well, all right. The last time I bought one it was an eight tall."

"Bingo!"

"I've won a bingo prize?"

Since returning from Madison last week, she'd been playing a game of her own, pretending to the world that everything was normal and happy in the life of English instructor Paine. Constance was her best friend on campus, but this call was grating on Hester's already raw nerves.

"Not exactly, but you have a chance to become a heroine in your own time. Peggy Greenberg was sent home sick with mono, which means she'll miss the Madrigal Dinner next week."

"That's too bad for Peggy, but what does it have to do with my dress size?"

"Peggy was playing Queen Bess."

Hester was trying to remember if she knew the student who was ill.

"She's the tall girl who braids her hair?"

"Yes, and the only one taking speech classes this semester who fits into Elizabeth's gown."

"Oh?" Hester suspected what was coming.

"You're the unanimous choice of the whole cast to take her place."

"Constance, I couldn't. A student should be queen of the Madrigal. Can't you let the dress out or shorten it or something?"

The gorgeous Elizabethan costume was the pride of the drama department, a gift from an alumna who'd worn it in a Broadway production. Since Hester had been at Halsted, it had been worn in the annual Madrigal Dinner by the tallest, slenderest student available.

"There's no way we can make it bigger without ruining it, and shortening it would just break my heart."

"But I'm not a student!"

"Bert Bellini always wears a costume to direct the Madrigal singers, and Bob Solaski is playing the Lord Chamberlain this year."

"It would be fun," Hester admitted. "Is it a big part?"

"You'll preside over the festivities. Your big formal speeches are the opening welcome and the closing. The queen can ad-lib quite a bit too. We will need you at the rehearsals, though." Constance was a little apologetic about asking time from a busy instructor.

"Every evening?"

"Not Friday. We're taking a break for the basketball game."

"And this weekend?"

"Saturday afternoon. I wouldn't ask if we weren't desperate!"

"All right, I'll do it. The dinner is a week from Saturday?"

"Yes, and we're sold out already! Thank you so much, Hester! I'll see you at Sadler Hall tonight at seven thirty."

"I'll be there."

Hester put down the receiver, trying to summon some

enthusiasm for playing the part of Elizabeth I. After her upsetting trip to Madison, it was just the kind of therapy she needed. The Madrigal Dinner was the highlight of the winter semester at Halsted, a re-creation of a Twelfth Night celebration in Elizabethan England. She'd attended the past two years, but this was the first time she'd been asked to participate. The speech department under Constance was in charge of the entertainment, little skits depicting life in Merrie Olde England. The Madrigal singers and the musicians playing authentic replicas of sixteenth-century instruments were the pride of the music department. Sadler Hall, the largest gathering place on campus, could accommodate over four hundred, and the tickets usually sold out weeks ahead of time.

The rehearsals did take her mind off Adam in the daytime, as she struggled to keep up with her classes and devote every spare minute to learning her part. By the time the big event arrived, she was spilling out *ye*'s and *thee*'s with all the command of a real queen.

Sadler Hall had been the gift of a lumber baron in his doddering old age, given not in penitence for the vast forests of the north devastated by his wood-hungry crews but as a memorial to his name. The marbled exterior was the gem of Halsted's campus, venerable and Grecian on its gently sloping site. The interior owed more to the Tudor craze that blossomed on architects' drawing boards in the 1920s, with a great hall two stories high and exposed beams that were blackened to appear aged on the day they were installed. Henry VIII would've felt right at home. No one on campus was old enough to remember, but most assumed that the hall had inspired the first annual Madrigal Dinner; it was a facility that demanded great happenings.

Hester came to Sadler Hall several hours before the time when guests would arrive, needing all the help she could get to put on her costume. Over the years the Madrigal wardrobe had grown into an impressive collection of padded breeches, elaborate doublets, lined capes, beautiful dresses, plumed hats, jesters' costumes, and peasant garb in fabrics as luxurious as velvet and silk and as utilitarian as wool and cotton, but none could compare with the queen's gown. The Elizabethans wore their wealth on their backs—gold, jewels, furs, and fine fabrics—and no one could look at Queen Bess's dress without being impressed.

The regal gown was a gingery-peach color, perhaps a bit faded since its debut on Broadway years ago, but all the more authentic-looking because of it. A heavy brocade, it hugged Hester's torso, made a V at the front waist, and flared out with such voluminous yardage that the skirt could almost hold her upright without having her feet touch the floor. The brocade was embroidered with gold and silver thread, and small glass gems sparkled everywhere. Slashed sleeves showed a gauzy silk undergarment, and a huge pleated ruff embellished with spidery lace framed Hester's head and décolletage. Her crown was a mound of colored stones sewn on heavy fabric with one large pearl hanging to her forehead. A knotted chain of pearls, large teardrop earrings, and a choker of red stones and more pearls were heavy reminders of the English queen's passion for adorning herself. The shoes and stockings were bright red, a favorite at a time when silk stockings were a fabulous luxury at the Elizabethan court.

Fully dressed, rouged, and powdered with her hair elaborately curled, Hester felt sinfully opulent. Imagine dressing this way at a time when a man's cloak might be valued at a year's wages! Queen Elizabeth's wardrobe had included thousands of gowns and accessories, more than even the luxury-loving ruler could wear, their number swelled by gifts from anyone seeking her favor. Hester could imagine her Calvinistic ancestors, somber in their plain dark garments, scorning the peacocks who strutted in the Elizabethan court. But for tonight she was going to forget those sober Puritans. She was the queen, and she looked it, elegant and commanding, her hair a halo of fire, her eyes alive with excitement.

"Your Majesty, we're nearly ready for the procession."

Professor Solaski, her department head, was elegant himself in a black velvet doublet with silver showing in the slashes. Not even black tights could do much for his legs, spindly and knobby-kneed, but he looked very much the

Lord Chamberlain with a heavy gold chain around his neck. His total baldness added to his slightly menacing demeanor, perfect for the part because anyone in Elizabeth's favor had to be a skillful intriguer. All Hester's reading told her Queen Bess had been a natural politician, not above using feminine charm to get her own way, but passionately fond of adulation, demanding and receiving constant flattery. How would it really feel to be the ruler of a nation, a queen with life-and-death power?

How would a woman like Elizabeth I deal with Adam Smith-Woodham? Hester bit her lower lip in irritation. She was too caught up in her part to let thoughts of *The Farewell Rock* spoil her evening.

A trumpet fanfare announced the royal procession. From a high platform in the midst of the long, cloth-covered tables, the Lord Chamberlain instructed the guests to rise for the queen, but sit immediately after she passed, so their honor wouldn't be bestowed on the courtiers and lowly people who followed her.

Hester felt like a queen, royally inclining her head to acknowledge her subjects. The momentary glimpse she caught of a man in a dark jacket at the far end of a table wasn't enough to identify him. She ascended to the head table on a raised platform, taking her place between Sir Walter Ralegh, almost as splendidly dressed as the queen, and the lords of Leicester and Essex. All the Madrigal company followed, standing for the queen's speech of welcome, joining in the toast with hot wassail that began the festivities.

The players at the head table, the queen and her court, were the entertainment, only pretending to eat at the banquet of wild boar, thick pork chops prepared by the college food service. The diners at the tables below them ate the first course, a hot, spicy baked apple, while jugglers and tumblers in bright jester costumes performed on the platform that served as a stage. Throughout the meal strolling players would move through the great hall singing, doing magic tricks, swallowing fire, telling jokes, and juggling. The *musica antiqua,* the group of musicians playing sackbuts, lutes, recorders, krummhorns, and other authentic replicas of sixteenth-century instruments, sat on a platform to the queen's right, while the Madrigals stood behind the royal party on her platform, singing when her majesty called upon them.

The feast began in earnest with the trumpeted arrival of the boar's head, a really astonishing papier-mâché creation spruced up with fresh paint every few years; no one remembered the artist who made it.

Hester perched on the edge of a high stool, all she could manage to sit on in the stiff dress, watching as plates with chops, huge chunks of butternut squash, and green beans dripping with butter were placed in front of each guest by waitresses in peasants' costumes. She surveyed her subjects and guests, her eyes riveted for a moment on the sandy hair of a man in the far corner of the vast hall. After a panicky moment of doubt, she forced herself to be reasonable; the huge chandeliers overhead were dimmed to a faint glow, making it seem that only the candles on the tables were illuminating the feast. In this faint light anyone might look like Adam. She had to put a rein on her imagination or she'd forget her part.

A rowdy good time was had by all as wandering minstrels kept the hall noisy. One knave, caught annoying the queen's lady-in-waiting, was sentenced to the Tower by Her Majesty, then sent to sea instead to sail for the glory of England.

Elizabeth I loved the splendor of her revels, sparing no opportunity to impress her guests. The steel of swords rang out as two gentlemen dueled for their monarch; one was carried out as the victor knelt to dedicate his victory to the queen. Hester nodded regally, suppressing a smile when the high-spirited student-dueler winked at her.

The trumpet fanfare sounded again when a flaming plum pudding was carried to the royal table. This prop was real, a dark rich cake loaded with fruit and decorated with white ribbons of frosting to be shared by the Madrigal players and musicians at the end of the evening. Each table received its own loaf, spectacularly flaming even if it wasn't the suet and fruit pudding of old, and a man at the end of one table was

45

asked to carve for his group. He played the host well, even though he was a stranger to those around him.

After the dinner plates were cleared and the pudding served, the entertainment began in earnest. Courtly couples danced on the platform, their hands uplifted and lightly touching, followed by rowdy peasant girls who romped through their routine then went out to the audience to flirt and squeal. The tempo of the music grew wilder, and the players began a lively dance around the hall, breaking ranks to press guests into joining their line. While the dignified queen watched, the man in the black cashmere jacket and turtleneck was pulled to his feet by a blond peasant dancer to join the growing string of revelers. Before the round ended, chosen guests from every table had joined in the lively romp, but Her Majesty only saw one man.

"I thought the tickets were sold out weeks ago," she whispered to Bert Bellini, lounging below her place at the table, waiting to direct the Madrigal Chorus in a final number.

"They were, but we had a few cancellations. Flu going around. I had a man literally badger me for a single ticket yesterday. Lucky for him you turned in your ticket when you got the part, so there was one odd seat available."

She wouldn't panic. This was her party! She could send him off to the galleys, and no one would know it wasn't another skit. No, it'd be better to ignore him; no guest would be rude enough to leave the great hall before the queen exited. Her costume might weigh fifty pounds, but it wouldn't stop her from slipping away from Adam.

Lost in thought, she hardly realized that the courtiers had begun another dance, this one stately and dignified, demonstrating it first, then choosing partners from among the guests. The platform and aisles filled with revelers, but one man lacked a partner and wanted one.

Adam bowed before her with artful humility.

"Gracious Majesty," he said loudly, "will you grant me the supreme honor of being my partner?"

"The queen does not dance," she said stiffly to cover her agitation.

46

"Would Your Majesty deprive her humble subject of the delight of her company?"

He was attracting attention, deliberately, she was sure, coaxing her with the honeyed words of a true courtier. Bert was amused, urging her to depart from the script. He signaled a stop to the music and announced, with the full power of his fine baritone voice, that Her Majesty would lead the next dance.

Theatrical makeup didn't hide the deep flush on her face as she was escorted to the floor by Lord Essex, with one elbow protruding to show off his brilliant green cloak, and handed over to Adam. With fingers uplifted and barely touching, they moved to a space cleared for them in front of the head table, and Bert signaled the *musica antiqua* to begin a stately number.

"Sir Smith is courting disaster," Hester whispered between clenched teeth.

"But Lord Woodham will dare all for love."

"His lordship makes a mockery of the throne." She felt his hand on her waist, warm through the thickness of the gown.

"Nay, Majesty, I only speak the truth."

"We like not thy truth." Hester hadn't practiced the dances; she had to concentrate to follow his fluid movements.

"Elizabeth has been known to change her mind—frequently."

"But not to wed," she said dryly.

"Ah, yes, the virgin queen! Dangling marriage alliances all over Europe but never coming through," he accused softly.

"I'm not dangling anything for you!" she said, breaking character completely. Her lips were frozen in a half smile, but her words were venomous.

"Under those regal rags there beats the heart of a Puritan," he said ironically.

"I seem to remember that they had their day, even in England."

"We all hope for at least a day in the sun," he whispered

inclining his head toward hers. "Your Majesty is uncommonly beautiful tonight."

"You shouldn't have come here," she said, losing her smile.

"I would've come sooner, but I had a few lectures scheduled last week."

"The question is," she said, nodding at the Lord Chamberlain, who'd claimed his own wife as a partner, "when are you leaving?"

"I'm not sure."

"If I were a queen, I'd order you banished now."

"Elizabeth was infamous for changing her mind," he reminded her.

"Only because she was cautious. She could be very firm, especially for the sake of peace."

"What's your price for peace?" he asked softly just as the music stopped.

"A great distance between us." She turned but couldn't, with dignity, avoid being escorted back to the head table.

Only the heavy dress was holding her erect; she felt like a rag doll left out in the rain, remembering with panic that she had a closing speech to give. Constance, costumed as a lady-in-waiting in a russet gown laced below an ample bosom, gave her the signal to end the festivities, and by some miracle she managed to deliver the queen's closing thanks to those in attendance, calling forth the performers to take a bow.

A spirited fanfare of trumpets brought the guests to their feet again as Elizabeth I passed from the great hall and scurried to the dressing room, not at all sure how she felt about her impromptu dance.

Why was Adam there? she wondered. Was he between books and bored, hoping for an affair to fill empty winter days? Maybe seeing her again had reminded him of their happy times together, rekindling some of the affection he'd felt for her. For a few happy moments she imagined a future with him, but it was a vision she couldn't hold for long. If Adam really loved her, he wouldn't have stayed away from her those long, agonizing months before his final separation from his wife.

The gown was a treasure and a part of the college's tradition, so she couldn't yank it over her head and discard it. Several of the peasant dancers had been assigned the chore of helping her dress and undress, removing the heavy dress with elaborate care and arranging it on a special hanger before helping Hester out of a silky shift and collecting her shoes. The red stockings were really a pair of modern panty hose dyed for the production; she was allowed to remove them herself. Unfortunately some of the dye rubbed off, giving her long legs a reddish cast that looked ridiculous with her unqueenly white cotton panties and a one-piece upper garment she'd had to buy to suck in her waist just a fraction of an inch for a safer fit under the queen's costume.

Slipping into a pair of lined navy wool slacks and a heavy gold sweater, she shivered and rubbed her hands vigorously. Sadler Hall seemed as drafty and cold as any Tudor castle to those who spent much time there. The great hall had been warmed by body heat and the excitement of the crowd, but the long, narrow room serving as the women's dressing room was chilly. She longed for a hot tub and a long sleep, but there was still the cast party. The queen had to cut the plum pudding.

The party ran late as the exhilarated college students repeated almost all of their acts with some rowdy variations for their own amusement. Hester forgot about being tired until she drove back to her apartment, parking in her designated spot in the rear and walking to the large porch in front of her entrance. A light snow had fallen earlier, blowing onto the porch, powdering the boards of the floor, and footprints led to her door and away from it. Russ was traveling with the team, and the paper boy certainly hadn't left such large tracks. What would it take to discourage Adam? What would it cost her to forget him?

"Want to talk about it?" Constance swirled a tea bag in the small metal pot, looking at Hester with concern.

"This will have to be a quick lunch," she said evasively. "I

49

have two appointments before my next class. Russ asked me to talk to one of his players who's having trouble. . . ."

"You don't have a class until three o'clock," her friend said with mock sternness, pressing the tip of her forefinger against her firm chin line. "Of course, it's none of my business if a mysterious man waltzes you. . . ."

Hester laughed, knowing when her friend was being theatrical. "The Elizabethans didn't waltz, and Adam isn't mysterious, only annoying."

"I wish some big handsome hunk would annoy me!"

"You could've had a Green Bay Packer, and you turned him down for this!" Hester gestured at the rather drab cafeteria, crowded now with town students and a scattering of faculty members.

"Well, there are hunks and there are hunks." Constance grinned, giving sparkle to her attractive face. "Who was that man in black?"

"Adam Smith-Woodham."

"Ummm, I've heard that name somewhere." She frowned in concentration.

"You gave me the notice for his lecture," Hester reminded her.

"You went to hear him and he followed you here?" Constance pushed aside the remnants of her tuna salad sandwich and leaned forward with interest.

"Not exactly. I knew him before I came here."

"You never said a word when I gave you the information about his lecture!"

"I'm not a name-dropper." Hester laughed weakly, but Constance wasn't buying her feeble attempt at humor. "All right, I met him when I was finishing my master's. We became friends, but he had a wife. That's about all there is to it."

"Does he still have a wife?"

"No."

"Ah!"

"Ah what?"

"Enter the Black Knight."

"Hardly!"

"He didn't come to Vienne to enjoy the balmy weather." Constance shivered and pulled her burgundy wool cape over her shoulders. "I swear they're trying to heat this campus on one lump of coal per hour."

"My classes were a little chilly this morning too."

"Chilly! The trustees should provide more heat or issue Eskimo parkas to the faculty. I could see my breath in play-production class."

"It can't stay fourteen below forever."

"No, it only seems like it will. What a woman needs in this weather is a nice warm body under a down quilt. I wouldn't mind hibernating for the rest of the winter—with the right man."

"Well, I certainly haven't met one." Hester felt cross with her friend, even though she knew it was Adam who was warping her sense of humor.

"I wonder," Constance said softly as Hester pulled on her coat, abandoning the larger part of a chef's salad.

Hester made a determined effort to be especially cheerful for the rest of the day, telling a corny joke remembered from grade school days to her afternoon freshman class. The joke fell flat, and so did the rest of the day.

When Sunday had passed without a sign of Adam, she'd been sure he was gone, but the following morning a large red envelope had been left between the storm door and entrance door of her apartment, a valentine from Adam.

The card was several weeks early and carried a blushingly sentimental message, along with a profusion of red hearts, cupids, and real lace. It had been hand-delivered; there was no stamp or address on the envelope. A personal message written in Adam's dark scrawl said: *Keep me in mind.*

She didn't need a corny valentine to remember the Madrigal Dinner! For a brief, giddy time she'd felt like a real queen, regal and in control, in charge of her own destiny. Untrained in acting, she had a natural flair for role-playing, throwing herself totally into the part. For a few minutes she'd wanted Adam to be her mysterious lord, her consort and lover. But she'd shed her role even before removing the enchanted dress. Adam might want their relationship to go

51

the way of Daniel and Jenny's in his book, but she wasn't going to play a part in his fantasies. Months of futile hoping, waiting for him to leave his wife, had left an only partially healed scar.

Her classes were beginning to moan a little, hinting that the assignments were longer than necessary. Maybe they were. Hester wanted to carry home big bundles of student assignments and give them exacting attention, trying to polish the writing style of students who could barely complete a sentence. Her better students received pages of encouragement and suggestions, helpful but puzzling to the recipients, who wondered if Ms. Paine spent all her time correcting papers. She did, almost.

The cold spell continued, at least bringing with it crisp sunny days. Hester left her apartment the next morning confident that her car would start; if not, she'd stretched her budget for nothing buying a new battery. In her haste to get to the campus, she almost missed seeing the white envelope pushed under the storm door.

If she didn't open it, she'd wonder about it all day.

This valentine wasn't as elaborate as the other, but the message, framed by delicate white doves on Wedgwood-blue paper, began with: *To My Beloved*. The poem was syrupy enough to be laughable, but Hester didn't laugh. She jammed the card and envelope into her purse, planning to shred it into tiny pieces as soon as she reached her shared office.

A student was waiting for her. Tammy Philips was a senior and one of the most conscientious students in the twentieth-century novel class. A delicate blonde with china-doll features, she made Hester feel awkwardly large, but her enthusiasm was sheer joy to an instructor who spent most of her time teaching required courses. Tammy was planning a term paper on women novelists between the world wars and wanted a list of authors that Hester had available. Her phone rang as soon as this student hurried off, and several other interruptions kept Hester busy until it was time for her first class of the day. Knowing the valentine was still in her purse made it seem as heavy as a load of bricks.

Adam was waging nerve warfare, she decided as she picked up yet another valentine on Saturday morning, the sixth that week. This one was almost as large as a magazine and had eight pages of romantic poetry from Shakespeare to Browning. The front had a white satin heart surrounded by gilded cupids and birds. Above his signature Adam had scribbled: *In my thoughts.* Hester flipped the card over and read the easy-to-decipher code on the back, not surprised that the valentine had sold for $3.50. If checking the price didn't prove that she was unaffected by his barrage of love messages, she didn't know what would.

The basketball team was home and playing a Saturday afternoon game. Russ had persuaded her to go with him to a faculty party that evening given by the dean of men. It was an annual buffet supper that she felt obligated to attend anyway. Other than that, the weekend was hers, free of papers to correct, as she'd slowed down on assignments, much to her students' relief. Later she'd have to go to the Laundromat, pick up cleaning, and do some shopping, but this morning she had time for a leisurely second cup of tea while she indulged in one of her favorite vices: reading lurid paperback mysteries.

Tossing the latest valentine into the little straw wastebasket by her writing desk, she settled back on the nubby seat of her brown-and-tan plaid couch, propped-up feet still clad in fuzzy green mules, arranged the skirt of her red-and-white flowered robe over her legs, and started to sip and read.

The doorbell disturbed her before the cup of tea was empty, and she automatically reached for her purse on the desk before answering, expecting to pay the newspaper carrier.

"Good morning. Did I get you out of bed?"

Adam filled her doorway, looking bulkier than he was in a heavy quilted nylon jacket that nearly matched the shade of his windblown hair. He rubbed his hands, slapping together the brown leather palms of his gloves.

"What are you doing here, Adam?"

"Freezing. I was waiting in my car until I saw you pick up

your valentine." He gestured at the New Yorker parked across the street half a block away. "May I come in."

Stepping back in resignation, she let the frigid air from the open doorway wash over her.

"Have you been here all week?" she asked.

"You missed me?" He smiled broadly.

"No, but I found your valentines. You're a couple of weeks too early."

"Or a couple of years too late?"

She only shrugged, wishing she'd gotten dressed.

"I paid a kid at the card store to deliver them. I had to finish my lecture tour, Champaign, Iowa City, Ames, St. Paul . . . Do you have any coffee?"

"Only instant."

"Fine." He unzipped his coat and hung it over the ladder-back chair by her desk, one of the few things she'd brought to the Midwest from her bedroom in Maine.

"I don't know why you're doing this, Adam. Just because we were friends a few years ago, doesn't mean—"

"I can waltz into your life and pick up where we left off?"

He sounded so damned confident. And cheerful!

"Something like that."

"You live here alone?"

"Yes."

"I thought so."

"It didn't occur to you that I may have met someone who's important to me?" Anger came easily because he stirred so many long-buried feelings.

"Only seven or eight million times in the last thirty-four months, three days, six hours, and twenty-seven minutes. But I figured if there was someone else, you would have used him as a reason to get rid of me in Madison."

"I should've invented someone." She was almost as annoyed with herself as him.

Walking into the kitchen, she filled the teakettle to heat water for his coffee.

"Why else would the woman I love disappear?" His voice was soft and deadly serious now, coming from the doorless opening that separated the small kitchen area from the living room.

"For many other reasons."

She thought of asking him to leave. He probably wouldn't go, and she'd feel foolish.

"You were a magnificent queen. As regal as Queen Bess ever was and much more beautiful. Her hair must have been just about that color when she was young, but not nearly so thick and glowing as yours." He came close, touching the unruly waves on her shoulders with both hands.

"Stop, Adam." She poured water over a teaspoon of freeze-dried coffee, slopping some over the rim into the saucer.

"You never were comfortable being told you're beautiful."

"It's the way you do it!"

"I'm not clever enough with words?"

"You're much too clever!" She tried not to think of all the moving love scenes in the row of his books on her shelf. How many of them were fictional?

She dumped the excess water from the saucer into the sink and dried the bottom of the cup before handing it to him.

"Thank you." He carried it to the small round table by the bay window, her favorite spot in the apartment, with a view of the neighbor's garden, now a solid white mass of drifts. "Your plants are doing well."

He had to brush aside a great mass of hanging spider-plant vines sprouting new growth on the ends in order to sit on one of the two plastic-upholstered chairs. Preparing a fresh cup of tea with the remainder of the hot water, she avoided looking in his direction, focusing instead on the clear glass tabletop and the cheerful orange-on-white flowered design of the empty chair.

"Join me," he urged when she remained standing and sipped at the too hot beverage.

"You shouldn't have come here to see me." She sank down across from him, still avoiding his eyes by staring at the pale brown liquid in her cup.

"Maybe not, but I'm here now."

There was nothing she could say to that.

"What are your plans for today?" he asked.

"I have a lot to do: laundry, shopping, errands."

"And this evening?"

"I have plans then, too."

"A date?" He didn't quite hide his disappointment.

"I do have an escort to a faculty party."

"Ah, yes, busy campus social life. A cocktail party?"

"No, dinner. I expect to be out late."

"You're seeing someone regularly, then?"

"Fairly regularly." One did see one's neighbor, and Russ sometimes dropped in to watch a game on her TV on the excuse that his was all gray fuzz.

"I just like to know the odds." He smiled ruefully.

"For us the odds are astronomical! A billion to one, a trillion to one." She couldn't remember what came after trillions.

"Oh?" He reached across the table and covered her slender hand with his. His thumb caressed the thin skin on her inner wrist, making lazy circles.

"Your pulse is rapid. I think that lowers the odds a little in my favor."

His knowing smile infuriated her! Of course she was stimulated by his nearness; she wasn't a store-window mannequin, and he was an extremely virile male. That didn't mean she could handle having him in her life again!

"I didn't know you had medical qualifications," she snapped, trying but failing to draw her hand away from him.

"A little sharp-tongued this morning, darling?"

He was spreading her fingers apart, keeping her hand palm down on the table, running one finger up and down the sides of hers, then caressing the loose creases of skin over her knuckles like a laboratory technician examining some exotic specimen. It was totally unnerving, but when she tried to free her hand, he clamped his over it.

"Do you begrudge me a little hand-holding?" he teased.

"Adam, go back to wherever you live now."

"When I'm not traveling, I stay at the cottage. You wouldn't want me to freeze my buns trying to survive at the beach this time of year with only one open fireplace for heat?"

"Frankly, I don't—"

"No, don't say something you'll regret."

"I only regret seeing you again! Adam, I like my life here. I'm up for tenure this spring, and if I get it, I may stay here indefinitely. This is a nice town, a good college."

"I'm not here to take anything away from you," he said soberly. "I just think we both owe ourselves a chance."

"A chance for what? Another big scene in your next book?"

"That's a pretty low blow, Hessie."

"Not as low as—"

He was standing, turning to leave.

"Well, good-bye, then."

He moved quickly into the living room, slipping into his coat as she followed him.

"The valentines were nice," she said awkwardly.

"As propaganda for my cause, they apparently bombed. You will get one every morning until Valentine's Day. That's all arranged." He turned to face her, zipping his coat. "Thanks for the coffee."

Watching him reach for the door handle, she felt wooden, wanting something but not knowing what.

"So long." He offered his hand for a shake, and she offered hers without hesitation.

Their palms never met. He drew her into his arms with startling quickness, beginning a no-nonsense kiss that went on and on until her token struggle turned to responsiveness. The coffee he'd been drinking made his breath richly aromatic, and she went limp against him when he covered her mouth with his and slowly siphoned the sweetness from her lips.

He could never kiss her without touching her hair, burying his fingers and bringing a silky wave to his cheek. His coat was slippery and even bulkier than her robe, but even with all the padding between them, she felt the long-remembered hardness of his body and was shaken by the intensity of her reaction.

57

"You have to shop today?" he whispered, opening the top of her robe to nuzzle the side of her throat.

"That's what I planned," she whispered breathlessly.

She went a little crazy when he slowly and methodically popped snap after snap on her robe, exposing the length of her serviceable red flannel gown. Unzipping his coat, she hugged his waist, parting her lips for a deep, satisfying kiss that didn't happen. He gave her a quick noisy buss, gently removed her arms, and walked to the door, leaving without another word.

The surprise quickly wore off, leaving her in a state of total rage. The high-handed arrogance of the man was unbelievable! How could he bulldoze her with passionate kisses one moment and walk away without a word the next? She was so angry—at herself! One kiss from Adam, and she was back to being the naïve, infatuated graduate student of years ago. How could he do that to her? How could she let him?

When her anger had cooled a little, she realized that Adam had done what she requested: He'd left. This might be his last attempt to see her. Right at this minute his New Yorker might be on the outskirts of Vienne, heading away forever. Certainly there was nothing to keep him in the winter-ravaged little college town.

On the rare occasions when Hester was depressed, she spent money. Unplanned spending sprees were as unusual in her life as orgies in the life of a nun, but today she threw aside all traces of her Yankee thriftiness and went to the town's one elegant women's shop, trying on everything in her size until she settled on an outrageously expensive, dramatically sensational silk crepe de chine dress. Pleated from the high neckline to the hem, it was a deep, vibrant turquoise unlike anything she'd ever worn. Full sleeves narrowed to tight-fitting six-inch-wide cuffs, and the pleats swirled in intriguing ways around shapely legs. She used her charge card because there wasn't enough in her checking account and knew she'd hate herself when the bill came. But tonight she wouldn't need to play at being queen. She was going to be eloquent in her own right.

CHAPTER FOUR

Homer Williamson entertained three times during the academic year, picking dates from the school calendar to ensure maximum attendance. Only a handful of professors, department heads who called the dean by his first name, were invited to every party. Associate professors and assistant professors summoned to the Williamsons' twice in one school year could feel fairly secure in their positions. Most were tenure teachers and weren't rocking the boat unnecessarily. A lowly instructor could only expect an invitation to one dinner party per year, and this was it for Hester. That she was invited at all was a good sign; her officemate, Brad Harris, was several rungs higher up the academic ladder and still waiting for his annual invitation, probably because he was vocal in wanting the faculty to organize for collective bargaining to obtain higher salaries.

Halsted College did have a president, but it was Dean Williamson who presided over internal affairs. Fund-raising was a full-time job for President Burnam, who was away from the campus so much that the faculty tended to forget about him.

"You look great!" Russ whistled through his teeth, complimenting Hester on her new dress, the sound unfortunately reminding her of a referee's whistle.

He looked sharp himself in a three-piece gray suit; unlike

some very tall men, he was nicely proportioned with a long, lean torso that matched his limbs. Just when she wondered if she should take his interest more seriously, he started talking basketball.

They were in the entry hall of the Williamsons' house, hanging their coats in a closet indicated by the dean's wife. Both were too new to the college to be late for the dinner, so naturally they found themselves the first to arrive. Mrs. Williamson had answered the door and pointed toward a huge room at the back of the house, inviting them to make themselves at home.

Everything about the dean's home was grandiose. Built by one of the town's founders in an era when gingerbread trim and stained-glass windows were more important than convenient plumbing or efficient heating, it had a dining room, den, library, kitchen, pantry, and game room on the first floor besides the high-ceilinged common room, as the occupants called their living room. The dean and his wife, alone now that four children had flown the nest, managed to live in Victorian splendor by renting third-floor rooms, originally used by servants, to students. The dean retained the illusion of privacy while reaping the benefits of a landlord, requiring his tenants to use the outside stairs, installed to meet the requirements of the fire marshal.

"We're early," Hester whispered, a little awed by the vast common room furnished with an eclectic assortment of antiques and modern pieces that included very few comfortable places to sit.

"No, we're right on time," Russ insisted, checking his watch, a complicated wrist piece that was accurate to the second and was often used to time players' drills.

They smiled at each other a little self-consciously and helped themselves to punch, fruity but strongly alcoholic, from a cut-glass bowl on a corner table, wandering around the room and looking at the dean's collection of oil paintings, most of them darkened with age. Russ was telling her about a high school senior in Oshkosh he was hoping to recruit for the team, when the dean, red-faced, rotund, and

60

dignified, bustled in and greeted them in his best jovial-host manner.

"Russ, Miss Paine, so good to see you!"

He always forgot her first name, but this time she hardly noticed. The two guests with him nearly made her drop her cup of punch.

"Bob's wife is down with the flu," the dean went on. He gestured at Dr. Solaski, Hester's department head. "Adam, these are two bright new people on our faculty here. Miss Paine is in liberal arts, and Russ Michaels is our new assistant basketball coach. Russ has been beating the bushes to bring us more topnotch players, right Russ? This is Adam Smith-Woodham, the author. I'm sure you've heard of him."

The dean couldn't even remember what she taught, but Hester was too stunned to worry about her status with the college administrator. She stared incredulously at the hand Adam offered her after shaking Russ's.

"Hester and I have met," he said smoothly. "She attended my lecture in Madison and told me some good things about Halsted."

He held her hand a moment longer than necessary, gently squeezing her fingers before releasing them.

"Adam wants to do research on a liberal arts college in a midwestern town for his next book," Bob Solaski said. "I'm trying to convince him that Halsted is typical, but unique enough to be interesting."

Her boss was beaming with satisfaction, so obviously scoring points by bringing a famous author to the dean's party that she wanted to scream. What kind of game was Adam playing now?

"I didn't know you knew Mr. Woodham," she said, talking directly to her department head and deliberately omitting Smith from his name, as though he was just a casual acquaintance and she didn't know about the hyphenated name.

"Smith-Woodham, but I prefer to be called Adam." He spoke quickly and flashed a broad smile at her.

"Adam just introduced himself to me today," Solaski admitted. "He's done some teaching in New England and knows an old friend of mine at Bennington."

He probably autographed a book for him when he was passing through Vermont, Hester thought ruefully, distrusting the good-old-boy network that made instant friends of males and made it possible for Adam to worm his way into practically any gathering of academics. The question was, What did he expect to gain by seeking out Bob Solaski?

"Delighted you could join us, Adam." The dean didn't like to have a conversation drift away from him for too long.

Mrs. Williamson made a belated appearance carrying a tray of hors d'oeuvres, offering them to each guest in a faintly apologetic way. She was a tiny woman, less than half the weight of her husband, and was easily overlooked in a group. Hester had tried to draw her out at their first meeting, but thirty-one years of living in the dean's shadow had narrowed Wilma Williamson's interests to the confining walls of her home. Hester felt sorry for her; accepting a hot shrimp puff, she praised it lavishly, feeling fervently grateful for her own independence and Yankee strong-mindedness.

The conversation soon shifted to the winning basketball team, the dean and his wife left the room to welcome more guests, and Hester moved over to the punch bowl, refilling her cup to cover the unease Adam's presence caused. Two more couples arrived and were introduced to the novelist, but Hester refused to be part of his audience, instead wandering into the dining room and through to the kitchen, offering to help Mrs. Williamson even though she expected to be refused. The dean didn't seem to trust anyone but his harried wife to handle the details of his triannual feasts; no matter how many guests were invited, she labored alone to carry off the dinner. Her offer of help declined, Hester went back to the common room, nearly tripping on one of the oriental rugs spread on the dark oak flooring. Adam was holding court with more newcomers, charming a biology professor, a paper technology instructor, and their wives. Russ was being advised on how to win basketball games by several armchair coaches. Give a man a Ph.D. and he's an expert on everything, Hester thought, not at all in a party mood now and feeling a little sorry for Russ. He couldn't eat lunch in the campus cafeteria without getting several lectures on how to run the team, and he wasn't even the head coach.

Refilling her punch cup again, she walked away from the sound of Adam's voice, going into the library, one room in the vast Victorian relic that she really loved. Dark walnut paneling and built-in glass-fronted bookshelves made the room a booklover's paradise. She liked to read the titles in personal libraries and analyze the owner's personality. This book collection didn't tell her much about the dean's interests; he seemed to have purchased his library by the yard, favoring sets of classics in fancy bindings. Hester was willing to bet most of them had never been opened.

"I wondered where you were hiding."

She spun around guiltily, feeling as if she'd been caught pilfering the silverware.

"Sorry if I startled you." Adam smiled broadly, pushing his hands into the pockets of crisp gray flannel trousers. As usual, he wasn't wearing a tie, the only man present who wasn't, but the soft white sweater was perfect with his navy blazer.

"What are you doing here?" she challenged in a low voice, sipping at the punch to appear nonchalant.

"My good friend Bob Solaski invited me."

"You never met him before today!"

"No, I learned his name at the campus library this afternoon. It's listed in the college catalog. English department heads are always very hospitable to authors. It was blind good luck that he brought me to this party."

"Why pretend you're going to write a book about Halsted College?" She drained her cup, feeling a little light-headed.

"Are you sure I'm pretending?" He moved closer, cornering her behind the dean's somewhat cluttered tooled-leather desk top.

"Adam, I don't understand what you're doing here, and I don't like it."

"Leave with me right now," he urged, "and I'll explain."

She saw his chest move with a sharp intake of breath and

knew his invitation wasn't a casual one. Unblinking eyes awaited her answer, and his intense scrutiny made her feel like squirming.

"I can't do that. The dean's party is a command performance. Anyway, I came with someone."

"Ah, yes, the basketball coach. He seems pleasant. And tall. Very tall."

"He's very nice!"

"He was telling me about a player he's trying to sign up in Oxcosh."

"Oshkosh!"

"Okay, Oshkosh. I understand he played Big Ten ball." He reached forward and took the cup from her hand. "Strong punch. I don't recommend more than one cup."

"I can set my own limits!" She took the cup back. "And don't pretend you're interested in sports, Adam."

"I am. I played a wicked game of junior tennis, and I plan to do some cross-country skiing while I'm here."

"Those are individual sports."

She knew he had little interest in playing team sports and even less in being a spectator. "You have to care who wins," he'd told her a long time ago.

"How long do you intend to be here?" she asked, draining the last drop from the nearly empty cup.

"Depends." He made a show of looking at a row of books bound in dark blue leather with gold lettering. "Wonder if he's cracked the binding on any of these."

She didn't tell him she'd been wondering the same thing.

"They'll be serving dinner. I shouldn't monopolize the dean's distinguished guest." She moved toward the common room.

"I won't jeopardize your chance for tenure," he said, smiling ironically and stepping aside. "But I do think that punch is too damned strong. The dean must know a lot about his faculty after one of these parties."

Just to spite him, she filled her cup again, carrying it with her to dinner. The table was banquet-size, covered with two huge white linen coverings, each of which had to require at least an hour of laborious ironing. Four card tables, two on

64

each side at one end, made wings to hold the overflow of guests. Name cards in little china holders marked each guest's place. Apparently sitting at the smaller tables was considered "eating below the salt," the place where people with no status sat in medieval times. Hester found herself seated at one with Russ, proving that basketball didn't have any real clout on the dean's priority list. In fact, she noticed, the head coach was missing from the gathering; apparently he hadn't attained three-dinner status, in spite of his winning season.

Adam was given the ailing Mrs. Solaski's seat, just two places down from the dean himself at the head of the table. There was a chair for Mrs. Williamson, but she didn't have time to use it. Why on earth didn't they hire a couple of students to help with the serving? Tenure be damned! Hester polished off the rest of her punch and excused herself to the paper tech prof and his wife, deciding to assist the hostess whether she wanted help or not.

After a token protest, the dean's wife let herself be over-come by Hester's insistence, gratefully allowing her to carry heavy tureens and platters.

The meal was incredibly rich, beginning with homemade French onion soup. Chicken breasts with slices of Canadian bacon and cheese were deep-fat fried, then baked and served with a thick sour cream and mushroom sauce. Twice-baked potatoes, the whipped filling loaded with bacon, onion, and green pepper bits, were served in half skins and topped with a cheese sauce. The cauliflower, broccoli, and carrot combi-nation was garnished with parmesan, and the salad came with blue cheese dressing and was topped with more of the blue-veined delicacy. Homemade rolls had buttery-brown tops, and Mrs. Williamson's preserves were thick with strawberries and peaches. Served on inherited china in a flowery blue pattern, the meal was overwhelming, and there were no small portions. The menu had been chosen by the dean, right down to the chocolate cheesecake, and he com-plimented his wife as he more than did justice to it.

Hester ate half of what she had on her plate and enjoyed none of it, too conscious of Adam's frequent scrutiny to be comfortable. Maybe she was a tiny bit tipsy; she was having trouble following the conversation near her.

"How soon do you think we dare leave?" Russ whispered. Mrs. Williamson had pressed a second helping of cheesecake on him, and he'd been too kind to refuse. "If I eat any more, my stomach will look like a basketball."

"We'll have to play it by ear," she whispered back, trying to pretend that Adam's warm brown eyes weren't lingering on her far too often for comfort.

Hester helped clear the dishes away, rather regretting that she'd worn her outrageously expensive new dress to play maid, then rejoined the crowd milling around in the common room, everyone too sluggish from the heavy meal to be very animated. Lucky Constance! She'd been tapped for this party but already had plans to take her play-production class to a Guthrie Theater performance in Minneapolis, an overnight excursion that the dean couldn't expect her to cancel for his dinner party.

Mrs. Williamson disappeared into the kitchen, unmissed by spouse and guests, and the men and their wives gradually separated, the women forming a group around a Victorian sofa dripping with carved grapes. The dean held court in the midst of the male Scotch drinkers. Hester was the only female faculty member there, except for the poetry instructor, who was an old friend of some of the wives, which left her at sea between the two clusters of people: her colleagues and their wives. The paper tech's spouse was very, very pregnant, and the women became carried away giving prenatal advice and recounting their own deliveries.

Dean Williamson played bartender for the men while his wife supplied coffee to the women. Hester didn't care for Scotch and certainly didn't need it, since she still felt a little fuzzy-headed from the punch and dinner wine, but she felt goaded by Adam's constant surveillance. What was he doing here? Needing to rebel against someone, she chose the dean.

"Scotch on the rocks, please," she requested, ignoring the dean's what-are-women-coming-to frown. Belatedly remembering that he had enough personal influence to put her tenure in jeopardy, she flashed a dazzling smile at him, hating her necessary hypocrisy. "Just a tiny bit," she added more cautiously.

He poured a hefty double, handing it to her with a forgiving smile.

Hester wandered back to the kitchen, but Mrs. Williamson had disappeared, summoned to answer the phone in a far section of the house.

"Maybe I should take you home." Adam lounged against the doorjamb, catching her in the act of refilling her glass from a partially empty bottle on the counter.

"I came with someone," she informed him, her words slurring together.

"Yes, the coach. You look lovely tonight. You should wear that color more often. But are you sure you want to get drunk here?"

"I'm bored, not drunk," she insisted, sipping the bad-tasting liquor.

"I blame myself. My coming here upset you."

"Certainly not, but I don't understand why you did."

"I'll come to your apartment later and explain."

"No!".

"You'll have company?" His eyes narrowed suspiciously.

"Certainly not!" Those words had a nice ring. She said them again. "Certainly not!"

"Hessie." He came close, resting his hand on her shoulder. "Let's end this charade right now."

"Only you can do that—by leaving. I can't believe you wangled an invitation to come here."

"It wasn't my idea, and I had no way of knowing you'd be here. We bachelors never refuse a home-cooked meal."

"Oh, Hester, you've helped me enough," Mrs. Williamson interrupted, coming into the kitchen. "You shouldn't be around my kitchen mess in that lovely dress."

It was the first assertive thing the dean's wife had said all evening. Hester tried to insist that she wanted to help with the dishes, but Russ sought her out just then.

"Hester, are you ready to leave? Mrs. Williamson, that was a wonderful dinner, just super. I explained to the dean that I have to be up early tomorrow. Team business." He inclined his head at Adam. "Nice to meet you."

"Good luck with your team," Adam said.

Russ's arm felt good around her shoulders as they walked to her door, but she was too concerned about not slipping, her high heels moving unsteadily on the slippery porch boards, to be prepared for the swift kiss he planted on her mouth.

"I needed that," he said, only half joking. "That dean throws a rough party."

"Especially rough on his wife," Hester agreed, feeling just a little disoriented.

"Can I come in?" His voice sounded thick and passionate.

She wasn't used to an amorous Russ, and her wits weren't what they usually were this evening.

"I don't think . . . I'm not feeling so great, Russ." This was certainly true; she rarely drank more than a single glass of wine, and things seemed woozy.

"Do you know what it's like living just above you?" he asked in a husky voice, leaning his arms on her shoulders. "So near and yet so far."

"Russ, we're only friends."

"That's not my fault!" He bent his head for a vigorous kiss that landed very wet and cold, since the temperature was hovering around zero again.

"Please, don't."

Accepting his invitation had been dumb, dumb, dumb. She should know better than to encourage an ex-basketball player who probably wanted seven-foot sons.

"You are one classy lady," he said, locking her against him with long, powerful arms.

"And I'd like you to let go, Russ. Please."

"That sounds clear enough to me." The masculine voice behind them startled Russ into releasing her.

"What are you doing here?" Russ demanded.

"I'm here by invitation," Adam said coolly.

"I see."

Russ looked at Hester for a denial, but she wasn't sure what to say. Both men sounded hostile, and she wished they'd both go away. Russ sounded mad enough to throw Adam off the porch if she gave him any encouragement. Whether he could or not, she didn't know, remembering the steel in Adam's arms and shoulders.

"I wish you'd both go," she said nervously.

"My pleasure," Russ said angrily, "Don't knock on my door the next time your car won't start."

It was a cheap shot, but it made her angry enough not to feel guilty. Russ went to the central entrance that led to his apartment stairs, leaving in disgusted silence.

"You go too," Hester insisted to Adam.

"Or you'll call the coach back to throw me off the porch?" he asked dryly. "I'm gambling that you're too civilized."

"You're anything but civilized." She realized that she was saying each word very, very carefully so the words wouldn't slur. "Can't you take a hint, Adam?"

"Hint! You've been bombarding me with rejection since the Madison lecture. If I believed you, I'd be long gone."

"Then believe me."

"All right. A good-bye kiss, then."

He leaned forward, lightly brushing her cold lips.

"You're freezing," he said, taking the door key from her gloved hand and opening the door, following her into the room.

"That was supposed to be a good-bye kiss." She started unfastening her coat, keeping her back to him, feeling peculiarly light-headed.

"Was it? Look at me," he said.

"She turned slowly, rolling love-crazed eyes in his direction," Hester said dramatically.

"What's that supposed to mean?" He sounded annoyed. She did look at him then.

"I'm helping you write this scene for your next book." She kicked off her shoes and went to the desk, fumbling for a sheet of paper. "We'd better write this down."

"Love-crazed eyes?"

"I know you like to make your scenes a little racier than real life. Now, let me see, your heroine will probably shudder like this." She demonstrated, hugging her arms across her chest. "Then she'll slither up to you and place your trembling hand on her bosom."

She moved very close, reaching out to take Adam's hand and lay it on the silky bodice of her dress.

"Oh, no!" She quickly pushed his hand away, realizing that the punch, wine, and Scotch had made her dangerously silly. "We'll write this scene without acting it out. It'll save hurt feelings." At least she was sober enough to know she wasn't quite herself.

"I'd like to talk about hurt feelings, but do you realize you're a little tipsy?"

"Now," she said, ignoring his question, "this is where your hero takes off his clothes. Slowly, of course. Give your female readers a little of the male-stripper bit. They're not really interested in how the woman's clothes come off."

She backed away, hands on hips, doing a few exaggerated bumps and grinds.

"You're living dangerously," he warned softly, watching the pleats of her dress shimmer against her slender length.

"But this is only pretend, Adam. You like games."

"Games I can win," he said ominously.

"Now, then, shall we use this room as a setting? The couch is a sofa bed, by the way. I like to be prepared for company. The curtains are a little faded. They used to be light orange and yellow stripes, I imagine, but the landlord isn't interested in replacing them. It's his carpet too: institutional green shag. The prints are mine, though." She gestured at two Gauguin prints, reproductions of lush and colorful island scenes with the dark-skinned natives he loved to paint in bright sarongs. "Some people are surprised by them. They expect me to hang barns and covered bridges and that kind of Yankee stuff."

She was talking too much, growing more animated as Adam watched with a cool, appraising stare. When he moved two steps closer, she folded her hands primly over her breasts.

"Will you describe these Gauguin prints in your new book?" she asked, trying to sound sarcastic but letting her hurt show.

70

"I still love you," he said softly, "even when you're in your cups and determined to make a fool of me."

"You're changing the subject," she protested weakly.

"No, it's been the only one on my mind since I saw you at the Madison lecture wearing that ridiculous hat. Did you really think you could disguise yourself with a hunk of fur and a pair of glasses?"

"It was worth a shot."

"There's no way I wouldn't recognize you. I even remember that little mole on the back of your knee. That wasn't in my book."

"Should I be grateful?" Her voice came out a pathetic little whimper as he came closer, within touching distance now.

"Adam . . ."

Everything was backfiring! She'd wanted to make him angry, to make him feel some of the outrage she'd felt reading the personal, private things in his novel. Instead she felt foolish and vulnerable, tripped up by her pride and acting ridiculous. It wasn't just alcohol that was making her behave this way. She wanted him! She needed to feel his arms around her, his lips probing hers and his hands stroking and loving her. Rubbing one nylon-clad leg against the other, she felt hollow, plagued with an emptiness only Adam could fill. She wanted him to make love to her, and he always seemed to sense exactly how she felt.

"Are you going to send me away tonight?" he asked in a throaty whisper.

His forefinger traced the sharp crease of a pleat beginning at the neckline, following it over the tip of her breast, making her weak with longing.

"I think you should go," she murmured, trying once more to deny her feelings, dropping her eyes to watch his lean, strong fingers find a pleat at her waist and follow it upward to her other breast, lingering for a feathery caress.

"You don't really want me to leave."

He was so sure of himself, and her head was swimming in confusion. How many times had she imagined the way his face looked now, concentrating on her so intensely that she felt drawn to him like slivers to a magnet.

"Come here," he ordered.

There had been very few orders in Hester's life. Her parents, firm, quiet people strongly believing in order and necessity, had suggested the right ways to Hester and expected her to acquiesce. Even now her superiors tended to make suggestions and comments, rather than give orders to her. Blind obedience was foreign to her nature, and so was this compelling, puzzling need for Adam. She moved one step closer, giving up something of herself in that small movement.

The width of a sheet of paper kept their bodies from touching. She dropped her arms to her sides, waiting in a daze.

His hands were big compared to her slender ones, but his touch was so gentle she shivered, sure that the stout cords of sinew that held her body intact would melt under his touch.

His fingertips explored her face, feeling the hard, smooth forehead, neatly formed nose, high, lean cheekbones, and silky-smooth complexion. When he traced the outline of her lips, she parted them, nibbling on his finger, astonished that it would occur to her to do so.

"Kiss me," he ordered, bringing his face so close that she could see minute bristles beginning to shadow his clean-shaven skin.

His beard before he'd removed it had been darker than his hair, silky under her fingers, curling exotically at the ends. She'd loved it because it was his; now she delighted in the hairless jawline and faintly scented skin.

"Kiss me now." His insistence was wildly exciting, a new facet of his complicated personality.

She obeyed again, knowing that she wanted to be in his arms no matter what the consequences. When she'd thought he was gone for good, she'd thrown away caution and good sense, buying a dress that was gorgeous and outrageously expensive. Now she knew she'd bought the vibrant turquoise creation for this man. She wanted to be stunning, enticing, erotic, as regal as any queen who'd ever lived.

Their mouths met in a brutal confrontation, betraying a hunger that shook them both. The same rash impulse that had led her to obey him was pushing her into total abandonment. His murmurs filled her ear as he crushed her against him, and she dug her nails into the thick wool of his jacket.

The room was whirling, but her senses were sharpened by expectation. She was a woman of the moment with no past and no future. All that mattered was the man who held her in his arms. He filled her world; he was her world.

Was it possible to want something for such a long time that when it came, fulfillment was totally divorced from reality? Her mind floated over the man Adam and the woman Hester, an observer of their frenzied needs. By the time her dress fluttered to her ankles, her spirit already belonged to Adam. The practical woman who balanced her checkbook to the penny every month and conscientiously corrected freshmen papers was somewhere else. She would've been embarrassed to see her slip hooked on the edge of a chair and her bra thrown on the desk. She'd blush when her panties, flimsy pink nylon instead of her usual white cotton, were hung on the lampshade and her hose dangled from the back of the couch. Fortunately she wasn't there.

"Darling, darling." Adam nuzzled her neck, running his hands down the curve of her spine until they rested on her round, smooth buttocks.

She was totally naked; he was fully dressed. It seemed unfair. Tentatively, because she'd never done this sort of thing before, she inched up his soft sweater, feeling the smooth skin over his ribs and the thickening mat of hair that ran from his navel to just below his throat.

"I think my jacket has to come off first," he teased softly, sliding it down his arms to the floor, standing as still as a statue while she inched the sweater up his torso, stopping to rub her cheek against his chest before she eased it over his head.

Just when she was beginning to feel a little foolish, more like the real Hester Paine confronted with an awkward situation, he finished undressing himself, sliding down slacks and shorts, kicking them aside along with his loafers and socks.

Sobering just a bit, she noticed how adept he was at shedding his clothing, then he pulled her into his arms. Her breasts pressed against him. Holding them in his hands, he bent his head to kiss them. Covering her shoulders and neck with slow, sensuous kisses, he made his way to her lips, parted in anticipation.

How warm he felt, his body locked against hers, broad and strong but not without little soft spots she discovered by wiggling against him and letting her hands roam. The hairs on his thighs carried tiny electrical charges, making her shiver and cling to his neck, then their mouths locked together in something more than a kiss. He lifted her against him, fingering her bottom, letting her ride his knee until she was sure she'd swoon with pleasure.

With an ease that amazed her, he scooped her into his arms, carrying her to the edge of her bed, leaving her for only an instant to toss aside the comforter, yellow and green squares of sturdy cotton tied with clumps of yarn. Lowering her to crisp white sheets, he dropped down beside her, taking her in his arms.

Murmuring words of love, he nuzzled her ear, her hair, and her throat, then caressed the peaks and valleys of her long, slender length, slipping his hand over and under her until she squirmed and giggled.

To her surprise and joy, he played with her, tickling her with his tongue, coaxing responses with teasing nips and feathery kisses, enjoying himself so much that his smile was as caressing as his hands. He made touching a delight, moaning in pleasure when she quickly learned what pleased him. His sensitivity made her love him without reservations; he instinctively understood that too much intensity, too naked a need, would frighten her. With leisurely gentleness, their bodies became acquainted. Aroused, their skin gave off a scent of yeasty sweetness more exciting than perfume, and the moistness of their contact made her feel as animated as a drop of water on a hot skillet.

"You're so lovely," he whispered, stroking the smooth skin of her tummy.

He was wonderfully strong, but it was a strength he controlled and husbanded, holding back to lead her to peaks of excitement beyond her imaginings. Sliding a thick down pillow under her hips, he hovered over her, then lovingly initiated her into the mysteries of passion. Slowly, gently, they became lovers.

Nothing she'd read or imagined was quite like this tender joining in flesh and spirit. Shocked in spite of her readiness, she dug her fingers into Adam's back until the trancelike rocking of their bodies became one undulating movement. His eyes were glazed with desire, then he shut them and took possession of her mouth, kissing her at the height of his arousal.

Woozy with wonderment, she abandoned the last of her restraints, closing her eyes to let a rocket carry her to unexplored universes. She came back to earth with Adam kissing the hollow between her breasts, laying his cheek there, sighing with happiness as a warm mound of flesh pillowed his face.

Feeling cherished and content, she smiled with tender pink lips, trailing her fingers over his torso, not quite believing that it was possible to feel so wholly at peace. When, at last, cradled on Adam's shoulder, she surrendered to sleep, it came like a black velvet veil floating over her mind.

She didn't want to wake up. Rousing slowly to remembrance, she felt unaccountably warm, then realized that she was locked against the source of the heat, snuggled under the quilt next to Adam's naked backside. What on earth had happened to her last night? Stirring slowly, she still felt euphoric, a mood not at all affected by a little stiffness and a mild soreness. Adam's leg was hairy against hers, with a pleasing silkiness she enjoyed so much, she rubbed her leg against his.

Moving very slowly and cautiously, she finally slid to the edge of the bed, a little surprised that she didn't feel at all embarrassed, even though this was the first time in her life she'd slept totally nude. She fumbled for and found her robe before looking down at Adam, still sleeping deeply. His hair was unruly and his face almost boyish in spite of the shadow of a beard, noticeable even in the dim light filtering through the blinds. She'd imagined waking up beside him so many times that actually doing it was strange but deeply satisfying. What should she say when he woke up?

She moved through the living room, picking up his scattered clothing and folding it neatly on the couch. Her own undergarments she quickly gathered to deposit in the bathroom hamper, only then giving attention to her dress so casually discarded on the floor. Bending over, she discovered, made a hammer pound in her head; if this was a hangover, it was her first and last.

She took out some clean underwear, a pair of black slacks, and a bulky red Halsted sweatshirt and hurried to the bathroom for a hasty shower, coming out to find Adam awake and propped up on both pillows, the sheet and quilt bunched around his waist. Without looking directly at him, she opened the blinds a crack and commented on the weather, overcast and threatening more snow.

"I didn't hear you get up," he said lazily stretching his arms above his head.

"I didn't want to wake you."

"Come back to bed, darling," he said, his voice enticing and husky.

"Wouldn't you like breakfast? I can fix some eggs."

She hadn't even considered eating until now, but it seemed a reasonable way to begin the day. Some strong tea might do wonders for her head.

"Come here first."

His commanding tone vividly reminded her of last night's scene in her living room, but when he reached out and enclosed her hand in his, she couldn't meet his gaze. In spite of her pounding head, she felt refreshed, renewed, but also shy about letting her feelings show. Making love with Adam had been indescribably wonderful. It could become more habit-forming than alcohol, which she vowed never to overindulge in again.

He pulled her close and planted a dry little kiss on her throat, pushing aside the loose, heavy hair to nuzzle her ear.

"You smell so fresh and sweet," he murmured.

"Wonderful what a warm shower will do."

"Are you hinting?" He laughed softly.

"No, I meant . . ."

"You mean that wasn't an invitation to shower with you?" He slid his hand under the thick sweatshirt, fondling one breast until her nipple grew hard under her bra.

"I think I'll get breakfast. Take a shower if you like."

Part of her was eager to crawl under the covers with Adam, but she was sober now, a little uncomfortable with memories of last night, even though she knew it had led to the most unforgettable experience of her life. Standing up, she smiled down a little nervously, unconsciously registering approval of the cocoa-brownness of his nipples against the golden hue of his skin and the fine hair sprinkled on his chest. She wanted to kiss the hard ridge of his collarbone and the smooth hollow of his throat, but the warm flow of desire spreading through her only hastened her retreat to the kitchen.

Making love with Adam hadn't changed anything, not really. She absentmindedly opened the refrigerator, her mind on the previous evening. She flushed just thinking about the way she'd goaded him, pretending to compose a love scene for his next book. Nothing she could write would come close to the excitement of making love with him, but where did that leave her now? She couldn't forget about the lonely months spent frantically wondering if Adam had changed his mind about loving her.

What did last night mean to Adam? With a trace of bitterness, she wondered if she'd read all about it in a sequel to *The Farewell Rock.*

She looked up to see him standing naked in the doorway.

"Is something wrong?" he asked quietly when she looked startled.

"No, of course not."

"Then come here and kiss me good morning."

"For goodness' sake, Adam, put some clothes on. It's cold in here." She tried to tease, but her voice sounded fretful.

"Oh?" He watched her through narrowed eyes. "I'm not in any hurry for breakfast."

Nudity was no big deal, she told herself, going through

the motions of putting water in the teakettle. Even movies showed naked men today. If Adam thought the past was forgotten just because—

"Do you like your eggs scrambled?" she asked, opening a carton.

"No."

She bit her lip, not looking in his direction, waiting for him to leave the room.

"Hessie." He stepped up to her, cupping her chin with one hand. "Am I supposed to apologize for last night?"

"Of course not." Her laugh was forced, and she dropped her eyes, finding it even more uncomfortable to meet his gaze than it was to stare at his body.

"Then what's wrong?"

"I'm not used to naked men in my kitchen."

"It is a little chilly," he conceded, kissing her forehead and taking her in his arms. "I need someone to warm me."

"Not this morning, Adam!"

He raised his brows, frowning and releasing her.

"Mornings are the nicest time," he said.

"I don't think so."

"Something is bothering you."

"No. No."

"Don't freeze up on me, darling."

"Really, Adam, I'm not the talkative type before breakfast, before my morning tea."

"And afterward?"

She shrugged her shoulders.

"I think I will get dressed."

He didn't hurry. She could hear the shower start and stop, but it seemed to take ages for him to dress. When he did come back to the kitchen, she was sipping tea and staring out at the snow-clogged expanse of her neighbor's garden.

"You look sad," he said.

His concern was harder to take than accusations or arguments.

"No. Maybe a little disappointed in myself."

"Because of last night?" He sounded hurt.

"Partly."

"You weren't that drunk!"

"You didn't take advantage of me, if that's what you think."

"Hessie, I love you. I think you love me. Where's the problem?"

Where was the problem? She should be glowing with happiness, feeling fulfilled and cherished. Last night she'd lain in Adam's arms, basked in his love, slept by his side. The evening had been everything she'd ever wanted with a man, and Adam's lovemaking was more wonderful than she'd imagined it. But this morning, in the cold winter light augmented by the neon glow of the ceiling fixture, he was still the man who had failed her. She hadn't wanted to break up his marriage; she'd allowed him to become close only because he and his wife were already estranged. Why, then, had he been so reluctant to come to her, if the marriage was over when they met? Why wait for his wife to leave him and then not even tell her about the final separation?

The answer was in *The Farewell Rock*. Their love had meant so little to him that he'd used it as material for a book. Maybe everything he did in real life was only research for yet another novel. Maybe she didn't know the real Adam at all.

Breakfast was on the table: fried eggs with bright yellow yolks sunny-side up and whites crispy around the edges; thick, dark slices of whole wheat toast; tall glasses of cranberry juice; and a squeeze bottle of honey.

"Well?" He was waiting for an answer she didn't have.

"It's hard to forget the past."

"I don't think it was bothering you last night."

"What do you want from me, Adam?"

"Your love."

She sat picking at the egg with a fork.

"Well?" he insisted, still standing and staring at her.

"It's not that simple! I can't just erase three years, especially not after all those months of waiting for nothing."

"You're young, Hessie! Do a few months really mean that much!"

"They did then, yes!"

79

"Rushing things isn't always the best way."

"It wasn't rushing things to want to know where I stood!"

"How do you think I felt when you started issuing ultimatums?"

"I hated feeling like the runner-up in a contest!"

"You were never that," he said angrily. "You were just too impatient, wanting everything right away!"

"That's not true!"

"Isn't it?"

His eyes were cold, but she was too angry to back down.

"I don't know why you came here! If you loved me, you wouldn't have tortured me. Not even telling me when your wife left you!"

"If you feel that way, there isn't much else to say," he said.

"No, there isn't."

"I'll go, then."

"That's best."

"But, Hessie, you are very, very wrong."

If he didn't leave soon, she was going to start crying. "Good-bye, Adam."

The door was shut with a dull thud; it was almost impossible to slam a storm door. The first hot tear squeezed out from under a clenched lid and rolled downward to dampen her cheek; crying was going to make her headache unbearable. She'd wanted him to leave, hadn't she?

CHAPTER FIVE

The wind stung her cheeks and lashed at her brow, making her head ache even more. On either side, snowy lawns and roofs sparkled with the brilliance of diamonds as the deceptive winter sun sent light but not warmth to the town. Walking had been a dumb idea, Hester admitted to herself, jamming both hands into coat pockets because her gloves weren't thick enough to ward off frostbite. A pair of high school boys carrying hockey sticks hurried past her, glancing for a moment at the grotesque fur hat that made her taller than either of them, blurting out "hi" self-consciously. People in Vienne were friendly; strangers automatically greeted one another when they passed on residential streets. Hester never regretted moving there, accepting the ups and downs of academic life with good-humored tolerance. Now Adam was turning her contented existence upside down.

Walking quickly now, so cold that her legs stung under lined wool slacks, she came within sight of the huge blue spruce that towered over her apartment, dwarfing the sizable bulk of the old house, now covered with yellow aluminum siding. As cold as it was outside, her cozy little apartment didn't seem like a refuge. She went inside reluctantly, knowing there was nothing there to distract her from disquieting thoughts about Adam.

Last night shouldn't have happened. She blamed herself,

not Adam, rejecting the excuse that she'd had too much to drink. In spite of his betrayal in using their most intimate experiences in the book, he still attracted her. Making love had seemed such a natural consequence of her feelings at the time, that she couldn't be sure it wouldn't happen again.

Her small living room seemed stifling as furnace-heated air made her chilled skin tingle. Hanging her coat in the front closet, she noticed absentmindedly that it was nearly dinnertime. Maybe she'd call to see if Constance had returned from Minneapolis with her theater group. Eating alone hardly seemed worth the effort.

The phone rang before she could make her call, and she dreaded answering it. If it was Adam, there was nothing to say. Admitting that she still loved him would be a terrible mistake; he'd be encouraged to stay in Vienne, and both of them would be hurt. She couldn't make an emotional commitment to a man she didn't trust. After listening to seven insistent rings, she reluctantly picked up the receiver.

"You're home," Adam said, sounding unaccountably relieved.

"Adam, I'm busy."

"Is the coach there?" he asked dryly.

"No." She wasn't going to use Russ as a buffer; that ruse was unfair to him and could only lead to complications.

"You're alone, then?"

"I can be alone and still be busy," she said crossly, wanting to make him angry. Maybe a heated argument was the best way to end things.

"I certainly can understand that. Have you eaten?"

"I'm just going to have a bowl of soup. I have work to do."

"A pizza is just as quick. Hold the can opener. I'm on my way." The phone went dead before she could protest.

She didn't want him to come over! He'd acted out the final scene in their relationship. Why couldn't he forget her and leave?

Either pizza service was unusually slow or Adam had changed his mind, she decided nearly an hour later. Fidgeting and pacing, she was torn between nervousness about seeing him and anxiety that he wouldn't come. Nothing was ever a sure thing with Adam! He wasn't unconventional in the way that men who wore ponytails and lived on brown rice were, but he always followed his own instincts, setting aside orthodox behavior when it suited his purposes. It wasn't out of character for him to say one thing and do another, depending on his considerable charm to make his actions seem perfectly reasonable.

Adam, will you either get here or say you aren't coming, she thought, seething at his lack of consideration. He'd insisted on visiting her again. The least he could do was be prompt.

She was turning off the heat under the teakettle for the third time when the doorbell rang.

"Doesn't the college feed kids?" he complained, handing her a huge flat box made for supersized pizzas. "The place was jammed."

"There's no food service on Sunday evenings," she said, just remembering that herself.

"Green peppers, sausage, and mushrooms, right?" He took off his storm coat and laid it over the end of the couch.

"Your fabulous memory," she said wryly.

"I can do much better. Do you know that you have a tiny mole—"

"I know!"

How could he bring up something so intimate the moment he walked into her apartment?

"Don't be ashamed of it. The little imperfections emphasize how beautiful the rest of you is. That's why women used to paste beauty marks right by their lips."

"History according to Smith-Woodham?"

"No, blarney according to Adam."

He followed her into the kitchen and opened the pizza box.

"You brought enough for four people."

"I'm starving. Somewhere along the way I forgot to eat today." He didn't sound so glib now.

"Bad bachelor habits, I guess." She stirred some instant

coffee for him with enough vigor to crack the cup. "When are you leaving, Adam?"

"You sound awfully sure that I am."

"Aren't you?"

"I'm not sure." He separated a slice of pizza with his fingers and bit into the soft crust dripping with strings of cheese and thick sauce. "Help yourself."

"Not sure about what?" she asked.

"My future. It seems to get harder every time to start a new book."

"I read once that criminals and writers have the same work habits." She bit into a piece of pizza, famished herself because she'd been too upset to eat all day. "Periods of feverish activity followed by long stretches of loafing."

"Sounds pretty accurate." He licked his fingers, then crumpled a napkin in one hand. "Best I've eaten in a long time. The test of a perfect pizza is whether it drips. If the grease doesn't run down your arm, it's strictly substandard."

"Really, Adam, no lurid descriptions while I'm eating!"

"You have some sauce on your chin."

Before she could react, he leaned over and kissed her, flicking his tongue against an imaginary spot below her lips.

"Don't!" he said sharply.

"Don't what?"

"You're going to run to the sink and wash your face, just on the off chance that there really is some sauce on your chin."

"You made it up?"

"Just testing the water before I took a plunge. The mood you were in this morning, I was afraid you'd play 'Yankee Doodle' on my head with a broom handle if I tried to kiss you."

"So now I'm a witch!" She tried to pick up another piece of pizza, but the topping slid off, adhering to the slice beside it. She stared dolefully at the empty crust and went to get a knife to recut the whole thing.

"Use your fingers," he suggested.

"A knife is neater," she insisted.

84

"Fingers taste better. Sometimes you have to grab for the things you want with both hands. Forget the messiness."

"Are you talking about pizza?" She finished recutting and nibbled delicately at another slice, wondering why fencing with Adam increased her appetite.

"I don't know what I'm talking about." He sounded weary and letdown. "You know why I'm here?"

"I don't."

"We're just a couple of old friends sharing a pizza, right?"

"Old friends?"

"You'd rather have me say lovers?"

"Acquaintances."

She reached for another piece. First she'd broken her all-time record for alcohol consumption, and now she was gorging like a pig on pizza. Adam certainly didn't bring out the best in her!

He laughed, but there was no humor in it. "Why would an acquaintance disappear without a trace, returning letters and all?"

"I'm talking present, not past." A thin rivet of oil ran to her wrist. "We should eat this with forks. Did you order an extra-messy pizza?"

He chewed a large bite, watching her with hooded eyes.

"Neatness counts a lot with you, doesn't it?" He glanced pointedly around her spotless kitchen. "You have the emptiest counters I've ever seen. Where do you keep the toaster?"

"On a lazy Susan in the corner cupboard. I don't like clutter."

"Clutter like divorces and ex-wives?"

"I was talking about my kitchen, which I use as little as possible."

Was this her fifth slice? She still felt a ravenous hunger. Maybe she was an obsessive eater and didn't know it yet.

"You've had enough!" He slammed the cover shut on the box with a vehemence that brought her hostility to the surface.

"I think I can decide that for myself!" She stood and glared at him angrily.

"At least I have your attention now!" Standing himself, he

leaned forward on the palms of his hands, challenging her over the width of the table. "Give me one good reason why you dropped out of sight."

"You were married!" She leaned forward too, palms on the table, then realized how ridiculous they must look.

"I was married when you met me. You knew it before we finished our first cup of coffee together!"

"And before we finished the second, you made sure I knew the marriage was floundering." She backed off first, sitting down, then regretting it because he towered over her.

"Did I ever once lie to you?"

"No, we've already settled that point."

Defiantly she threw open the box and picked up another piece of pizza. "And don't tell me what to eat!"

"Don't try to change the subject." He sat down with a thud. "We were talking about why you disappeared."

"You were talking about it."

She took an overly large bite and was punished by a trickle of grease that ran from the corner of her mouth. Adam saw it and snorted before she could wipe it away.

"Well?" He stood again and restlessly paced the length of the kitchen, hands thrust into pants pockets.

"I wasn't sure you'd ever be free." The rich sauce left a sour coating on her tongue and she felt slightly ill. "I needed to get on with my life."

"You don't erase five years of marriage like you do scrawls on a chalkboard. There are settlements, lawyers, decisions."

"When did you make the final decision?"

"It was made for me," he admitted grimly.

"Before or after I stopped writing?"

"Why does that matter?"

"It matters to me, Adam."

"Before, I suppose." He sat down heavily.

"But you didn't tell me."

He ran the fingers of one hand through his hair, frowning but not answering.

"Adam, why didn't you tell me?" she insisted, steeling herself to hear the terrible truth that he hadn't been in love with her.

"I don't know how to explain."

He sounded miserable, but she couldn't feel any sympathy for him, not when she was dying inside.

"Just tell me the truth."

"I don't know what the truth is, Hessie. I felt empty, drained. I needed time."

"But you said you loved me," she whispered.

"That's why I couldn't inflict myself on you then. I thought it would only upset you more to—"

"Upset me! Don't you know that dangling on the fringe of your life upset me? Not knowing where I stood upset me!"

"Darling, I solve problems a lot slower in real life than I do in my books."

"I was a problem to you?"

"No, never! I just wanted to be a whole person when I came to you. For that I needed time."

"You still loved your wife." Her own words hurt her.

He shook his head sadly. "No, the person I'd become couldn't love the person she'd become. But there were memories—things that had to be laid to rest. How can I make you understand it didn't have anything to do with you?"

"You wanted to isolate me, keep me in one tidy compartment of your life."

"That's not what I was trying to do! I needed time. If I didn't communicate well . . ."

"But you make your living communicating! All I was hearing from you was a career rundown. For all I knew, you could've been writing to me and sleeping . . ." She flushed, aghast at the depth of her resentment.

"Sleeping with my wife? No."

He slumped back on the chair, legs stretched out and hands gripping his thighs, looking like a man who had just been kicked.

"I didn't mean it quite that way." She couldn't look at him.

"Of course you did. I should be flattered that you cared enough to be jealous." His voice was toneless. "I did think you trusted me a little more than that."

Fighting back a rush of guilt, she remembered other things.

"I trusted you once. I certainly didn't expect you to write a book about our most personal feelings."

"I wrote about a woman I loved. I thought she loved me. Now I'm not so sure."

"That is so unfair!" She knocked aside the chair and ran to the living room, clenching her hands on the hard wooden back of the desk chair.

"Hessie!" He followed, challenging her from the middle of the room. "Listen."

"I have been. And my name is Hester. Hessie makes me sound like the monster in the Scottish loch."

"Don't be ridiculous."

"Me ridiculous?" She turned to face him.

"The resentments we're carrying around are a lot of excess baggage," he said. "What's past is past. I want to know what happens next."

"Nothing."

"After last night you're going to have a hard time convincing me of that!"

"Last night was a big mistake. It shouldn't have happened."

"It should've happened much sooner!"

"You may save your plots by having your characters hop into bed, but it doesn't work in real life, Adam!"

"Save my plots! You're on shaky ground there, sweetheart. You don't have to like what I write, but you sure as hell aren't qualified to knock my plotting. What have you ever written?"

"I'm more than qualified to evaluate literature!"

"When you grow up, maybe!"

"Why don't you leave me alone? I came here to get away from you."

"I think you came here because you're afraid of me. You might have to take a few risks to be my woman."

"Your woman! Next you'll want me barefoot and pregnant, waiting on my lord and master!" She was so angry she didn't care what came out of her mouth.

88

"Interesting idea," he said. "Especially after last night. But, darling, don't try to throw any feminist rallying cries at me. I prefer independent women. My mother refused to get married unless she could keep her own name, and that was before women's lib."

"Get out."

"Gladly, but not before I do what I came to do."

He slowly advanced toward her, giving her time to anticipate and counter his move, but she was paralyzed, drained by their first really heated argument. She willed herself to become so rigid that she'd be a statue in his arms.

Running his hand from her shoulder to her wrist, he took her limp fingers and brought them to his lips, slowly kissing each one while she watched in frozen indecision.

"Maybe," he said slowly, "we've hurt each other enough."

She didn't know what her answer should be. It wasn't in her nature to let anger destroy love; if anything, rage was a seasoning for passion, and she was more attracted to him than ever before. His hand was warm, holding hers in the way an awed schoolboy would cradle a wounded bird. She wanted to take back some of the things she'd said and forget all his angry outbursts. Life would have been so simple if they'd met as children and married as young lovers. He was right about carrying excess baggage in their relationship, but her emotions wouldn't let go of it.

"Maybe," she said slowly and doubtfully, trying to convince herself, "you should go."

"I plan to."

His actions belied his words as he slowly drew her into his arms, pressing her face against his, holding her inert against the firm length of his body. He wasn't aroused, and she was. It was a peculiar kind of humiliation to know he had that power over her, coupled with self-control on his own part.

His kiss, when it finally came, was leisurely and undemanding, sampling instead of consuming. He separated from her without a word and found his coat, putting it on in total silence.

She'd asked him more than once to leave, and now he

was. She wasn't sure what to do about it, but his attitude was making her miserable.

"Good-bye, Hester."

"You're leaving?" That was obvious; she wanted to know if he was leaving town.

"Obviously."

"Good-bye, then."

He didn't give her a chance to show him to the door. Watching him walk across the board floor of the porch, down the concrete steps, and over to his car, she felt as if her life were going down the drain.

Sinking onto the couch, she stared with sightless eyes at nothing in particular, trying to sort out the muddle of conversation that had passed between them that evening. They were like fencers scoring points by wounding. Now he was probably gone for good, and that prospect was unbelievably bleak. She could cry when she was angry, hurt, or sad. Total devastation left her dry-eyed and numb. She might have sat all night, torturing herself with regrets and old resentments, if it weren't for the pizza. Her stomach felt as precarious as a balloon filled with live crabs. She finally had to get up to rummage in the bathroom medicine cabinet for an antacid, but there wasn't any, because she usually could eat anything. She had to settle for a cup of warm milk, bland and tongue-coating. Grinding up the leftover pizza in the garbage disposal, she hoped never to see or smell another piece.

Talking with Constance a few days later, Hester didn't need much encouragement to tell her about Adam. She couldn't seem to keep her mind on anything else, and discussing the whole situation with a sympathetic friend was the outlet she needed.

"So you see," Hester said over an untouched luncheon, "if you read his book, you'll know all about us. At least until he let his imagination run amok."

"You really wanted him to leave town?"

Leave it to Constance to zero in on the real dilemma!

"I don't know! Once I thought we'd be together forever as soon as he made the break with his wife. But he never left her. She left him. How can I be sure he doesn't regret the divorce? How can I trust him?"

"You could take a chance," Constance suggested without much conviction. She'd often discussed her love life with Hester but wasn't used to being the counselor herself. "What can I tell you? You always seem to know exactly what you want from life."

"Sure, the smart kid on the block." She was feeling sorry for herself and knew it. "Maybe I outsmarted myself this time."

"It's the college life," Constance said, shaking her head. "We get used to this orderly little world and don't want to take risks anymore. Seeing the play Saturday night, I kept thinking: There could've been a part in it for me. But what would one good part mean compared to a steady job doing something I like?"

"With tenure," Hester added.

"And eager young kids wanting me to tell them how to act like professionals. Great for the ego—sometimes."

"Would you really leave teaching?"

"That's the big question. I've had an offer."

"A part in a play?"

"Yes, in the touring company of *Wings of Love.*"

"Constance, that's wonderful! Are you going to take it?"

"I just don't know! I worked with the director in summer stock, and he's really good. It's such a great opportunity, I don't know what to do."

"When do you have to decide?"

"Next month. I can take the part and still finish the semester here."

"Any chance of a leave of absence?"

"Maybe, but would I want to come back to all this after touring with a top company?"

"It might seem pretty tame," Hester agreed.

"Security or the bright lights?" Constance gave her a humorless grin. "Should I stay here and be the professor or chance being out on the street after one season?"

"I hope you're not asking me! I don't even know whether I want to be in love."

"Do you have a choice?"

"Not much. But I put Adam out of my life once; I can do it again. There's not much choice if he's really gone for good."

"I've done the same thing, only my love is the theater. Did you know I had a part on Broadway?"

"No, you never told me!"

"The play closed the first week. Fizzled after a promising opening."

"That sounds like my romance with Adam."

"Well, I have a class." Constance drank the last of her tea and stood up. "Sorry I can't stay longer to watch you not eat your lunch."

"Thanks for listening to me, Constance."

"Hey, you're always listening to me! I probably helped you about as much as you helped me."

"So, we're big girls, and we have to make our own decisions, right?" Hester smiled, feeling more cheerful.

"You've got it! But sometimes it would be awfully nice to have a big strong man to lean on just a little."

The valentines came every morning. One was a foot high and showed a bear with a humorous verse; another had a padded velvet heart, shot through with a golden arrow. She started saving them, dropping them in a desk drawer, pretending it was only because they were too pretty to discard.

If Adam was still in Vienne, she'd know it sooner or later. The town wasn't tiny, serving as the site for numerous small factories and a concern that processed dairy products, but it was compact enough for word to travel fast. Bob Solaski would be sure to mention it if he saw the famous author again.

On the morning of Valentine's Day she dreaded opening her door, putting it off until the time when she had to leave for the campus. Considering all that had been delivered during the past weeks, it would be difficult for Adam to send a more elaborate card.

She didn't know whether to be disappointed or relieved that there was nothing between the two doors. Sending the valentines had been a meaningless gesture, robbed of significance since Adam had arranged for their delivery before he left. It was silly to feel so let down. Valentines were for kids anyway.

The bitter winter days seemed a thing of the past on this clear, sunny morning, still crisply cold but pleasantly so. She had some work to finish at the office before her first class; even as she became more experienced, she liked to prepare her lectures with care. Bored students didn't learn very much.

Shared offices were a constant source of irritation for the faculty, particularly since the typical one was only slightly larger than a closet and furnished with oversize oak furniture that had achieved antique status but left little room for moving around. Fortunately, Hester and Brad Harris were congenial officemates for the most part. She often wished he'd organize the mountain of clutter on his desk, and he'd once asked her not to dust his side of the room, a chore rarely performed by the maintenance staff. This morning he met her in the hallway with a real problem.

"They're gorgeous," he said wiping at swollen red eyes, "but I'm allergic, Hester. They'll just have to go!"

"What are you talking about? Shouldn't you be home in bed with that cold?"

"It's not a cold! It's roses!" He opened the door with a dramatic gesture, looking like a rumpled carnival barker in a bold green plaid jacket. "You've got to get them out of there."

The arrangement was a huge floral fan with dozens of deep red roses and small white carnations. It had a magnificence usually reserved for the winning horse on Derby day. Spanning the scarred length of her desk, it was completely overpowering in the little office.

She reached for the card, only dimly aware of Brad's stream of protest from the corridor, and recognized the bold scrawl even before she focused on the words: *Thinking of you with love, Adam.*

He'd written the card himself, but that meant nothing. Probably he'd made arrangements for the flowers at the same time as the greeting cards. This was only the finale in his parade of valentines.

Brad sneezed violently in the doorway, reminding her that she couldn't, in good conscience, leave the flowers there to torment her suffering colleague.

"I haven't time to take them home," she said, wondering if she could carry them by herself.

Feeling as self-conscious as a chorus girl at a school board meeting, she blindly carried the huge spray down to the lounge, putting it in the middle of the table where faculty members congregated for coffee. The room was mercifully empty, so she quickly removed the card and abandoned her biggest valentine, hoping she could secretly spirit it away after her last class.

Brad, it appeared, should've gotten his degree in broadcasting. By noon the campus buzzed with news about Ms. Paine's roomful of roses, and even her department head cornered her in the cafeteria.

"Quite a bouquet of flowers, Hester. Do we know the sender?"

She hated it when people used the royal "we."

"Oh, I don't think so," she said, walking on eggs with the man who, more than anyone else, held her career in his hands. He and his wife were good friends, often inviting her to their home, but when she had her tenure, she was going to find a tactful way to suggest that his pile hat with earflaps made him look like a Russian street sweeper.

"Lovely arrangement. Did it come from a local florist?" he asked.

He'd noticed that the card was gone!

"Yes, I believe it did. I wanted to ask you about the schedule for midterms. . . ."

She quickly invented a question and was relieved when a chemistry professor called Solaski away.

Carrying the flowers home was another problem. She begged two secretaries and a clerk in the registrar's office to take some of the blooms just to reduce the sheer bulk of the spray, but all refused. Was there some superstition about secondhand valentine flowers? Everyone said the arrangement was too romantic to break apart. If they only knew!

The stems were embedded in florist's foam, but someone had thoughtfully added water while the flowers sat in the lounge. Hester discovered this while carrying them to her car; trying to open a door in the building, she accidentally tipped the holder and sent a stream of water down her leg and into her boot. The temperature had dropped, and wet nylon froze to her leg while the boot made squashy sounds with every step.

At first the bouquet seemed wider than her car, but she managed to put it in the luggage area behind the backseat, grateful that her compact had a hatchback instead of a conventional trunk. She broke three stems loading them, but the flowers filled the space so completely that tipping over was impossible. Backing up the car was tricky; she had to rely on her side mirror because the rear was blocked by bobbing roses and carnations. She felt as conspicuous as a Rose Parade float.

Russ had been avoiding her, which made it much easier to avoid him. Unfortunately this had to be the one day when fate threw them together. His Buick chugged into the parking place beside hers just as she was struggling to remove the flowers. Part of the greenery had already toppled, and she'd never felt less romantic about a gift.

"Marriage or funeral?" Russ asked caustically, watching her struggle for a minute until his chivalrous instincts forced him to help. "Let me get it. You're knocking it apart."

He poked his arms into the rear of the car beside hers, and retreat seemed safer than argument.

"Just hand them to me, please," she said.

"I'll carry them to your door."

"Well, thanks." She shut the hatch door and followed him, walking cautiously because her wet leg was totally numb.

By the time she reached the door, her key was ready.

"Impressive," Russ said, ignoring her hands outstretched to take the display. Walking inside, he put it on the coffee table. "I don't see a card."

"No," she agreed. "Thanks for carrying them."

"Hester . . ." He wandered around the room, studying the flowers from different angles. "There's no reason why we can't be friends, is there?"

"No, of course not. I hope we are friends." She also hoped he wasn't going to ask her out.

"Good. Well, I'll be on the road recruiting after the play-offs, unless we go to the finals. Would you mind feeding my fish? I think Mrs. Carton overfeeds them. One died during our last road trip."

"I'll be glad to."

"Nice flowers," he said. "Roses were selling for thirty-five dollars a dozen, last I noticed."

"Let me know when you want me to feed the fish."

"Yeah, I will. I've got the directions written out."

Was he impressed by the flowers or just curious about the sender? Either way, he dallied and made small talk, finally saying good-bye cordially. She didn't have any inclination to feud with her neighbor, so she appreciated his friendliness, if not his lingering curiosity.

The container was still dripping, she found when she checked, soaking several magazines on the table. She lugged the flowers to the kitchen table, dried and polished her coffee table, and wiped dry the large plastic boat holding the flowers before returning the display to the living room. When the doorbell rang, she hoped it wasn't someone else who'd be curious about her huge spray.

"Happy Valentine's Day."

"Adam!"

"I see you got my last valentine." He stepped into the room uninvited and walked to the flowers. "Smaller than I expected, but they did a nice job arranging them."

"Smaller! My office partner nearly died of rose allergy, and they barely fit in my car. Why did you send them to the campus?"

"For your gratitude and thanks. I didn't think you'd be home to accept a delivery here during the day."

"Thank you," she said, knowing he was deliberately making her feel like an ingrate. "But they're too much, Adam!"

"I couldn't just send another card."

"You didn't need to send anything! I thought you'd left."

"I did, temporarily. My publisher seems to think I have to promote my book to sell it. I'm back now."

"So I see."

"Have you had dinner?"

"Yes."

"When? Your last class didn't end until five."

"How do you know that?"

"The schedule is posted in your office. Harris will live, by the way. He was pink-eyed and red-nosed, but he told me all about the flowers. I apologized to him."

"You told him you sent the flowers?"

"It was that or let him believe that Dan Cupid distributes Valentine's Day flowers to stricken maidens."

"I'm not stricken!"

"You're a sweetheart, though. I missed you." He moved closer and kissed her loudly on the cheek. "Did you miss me?"

"Certainly not!"

"You're a lousy liar. Where shall we eat?"

"Adam, I'm not at your beck and call whenever you happen to pass through town."

"I'm not passing through."

"What do you mean?"

"I've moved here. That's one of the reasons I came for you, to show you my house."

"You've rented a house?"

"No, there wasn't much for rent. I bought one."

"You're not serious?"

"Aren't I? Do you want to change into something more comfortable, or are you ready to go see it?"

"This is a practical joke, right? You've decided to celebrate Valentine's Day and April Fools' Day at the same time?"

"No. I haven't had time to put stuff away. The house is pretty unsettled. I recommend old clothes."

"I'm going to call your bluff!"

"You can try, sweetheart."

She hurried into the bedroom to exchange her still damp hose for a pair of Black Watch plaid slacks and an emerald-green sweater, slipping on her casual yellow nylon car coat. Adam was up to something, and she wanted to find out what.

CHAPTER SIX

A small, sluggish river, frozen solid now, cut the town in half, with the campus nestled on one side and the business and industrial areas on the other. The houses close to the river on the college side were large and Victorian, many converted to apartments like the one where Hester lived, while ranch-style and split-level homes sprawled on the fringes of town. Adam drove across the river on the Main Street bridge, south past a strip of fast-food restaurants, motels, and gas stations, and turned into a neighborhood of neat pillbox homes. Another turn took them into an older neighborhood of modest houses built in the 1920s and 1930s.

The New Yorker pulled into a narrow driveway, two concrete tire tracks with snow-covered dirt between them. The house that went with the drive had been called a bungalow when the architect drew the blueprints. Hester didn't know what to call it now. Skeptical before, she was absolutely incredulous when she saw the squat stucco house painted a rosy pink now dulled and soiled with age. A realtor's sign half buried by snow was pasted over with the word SOLD.

"You didn't buy this?"

"Sure I did. It needs a little paint and a few repairs, but I think we'll be very snug here." He grinned broadly and came around to open the car door for her.

"Adam, if you think this is going to be your little pink love nest . . ."

"I couldn't have put it better myself."

"You can count me out!"

"No, I can't," he said more seriously, leading the way up concrete steps, newer than the rest of the house, to a sun porch glassed in with storm windows but cold and musty-smelling. In one corner a dead and frozen snake plant drooped on a wicker fern stand, the white paint gray and peeling.

"This will be my summer office," he said. "With a reed mat on the floor and some sunscreens, it'll do nicely. I can soak up life in Middleville, U.S.A. while I sit out here typing." He unlocked a door to the house.

"You're just crazy enough to buy this place, aren't you?" she asked, still not wanting to believe him.

"I have a few ideas for the living room too," he said, stepping directly into a fair-sized room that spanned the front of the house. "Don't judge it by the way it looks now."

"I'm not judging it. I think it's insane to buy any house in Vienne. What will you do with the beach house?"

"Use it as a summer cottage, the way I always have. The furniture I brought here is from my apartment in Boston."

"I didn't know you were living in Boston," she said half to herself.

"You would have, if you'd kept up your correspondence with a certain old friend. The room has possibilities, don't you think?"

A large stone fireplace dominated the room, made not of smooth boulders but of rocks split to reveal their full natural beauty and fitted together by an artist.

"The fireplace is a treasure," she said spontaneously. "I've never seen stonework quite like that."

"The realtor said there are several like this in town, but the mason worked mostly in northern Wisconsin. Died young, unfortunately. He had a drinking problem, so contractors couldn't depend on him. When he was sober long enough, he did work like this."

"I still don't understand why you want a house, but I begin to see why you bought this one."

"It needs a bit of redecorating, that's all."

This was an understatement. The rug was a drab solid brown, a virtual magnet for light-colored threads and bits of lint. The walls were a greasy-looking green, painted before latex colors were used in homes, and the drapes were originals, dusty tan with splotches of color that had once been burgundy and navy flowers. Except for a card table and two folding chairs, the room contained only unopened corrugated cardboard boxes.

"I didn't get any living room furniture in the divorce settlement," Adam explained a little sheepishly. "I've been meaning to get some, but I'm not home much."

"Exactly! You're not home much! You shouldn't have bought a house."

"I can decide that for myself." He didn't try to disguise his irritation.

"Well, show me the rest."

She felt just a little chastised. Adam had reason to be annoyed; she didn't have any right to tell him what he should or shouldn't buy.

"I've never seen a house quite like this," he said. "It's more like a cabin than a town house, no halls or entryways. Those two doors lead directly into the bedrooms."

"Right off the living room. It's an unusual floor plan."

"And the kitchen's through here. The bathroom has two doors. The other goes into a bedroom." He led the way, giving her a glimpse of rooms with cracked linoleum floors and walls painted faded shades of peach and yellow. "The second bedroom only has a door opening into the living room."

"Cozy." She felt much less comfortable and much less critical seeing the furnished bedrooms. The room with the bathroom entrance was unorganized but definitely an office, with an electric typewriter sitting on a metal stand.

"I'm going to get a word processor. The way I revise, it should cut my writing time in half."

He gave her a steady, challenging look, but when she said

101

nothing, he led the way through the living room into the only other room, the second bedroom. A standard double bed with matching dark walnut dresser and chest were crowded into the room. With a Hudson Bay trading blanket —thick white wool with bold stripes of red, green, and yellow—covering the bed, the room was the only settled-looking one in the house. It also made Hester the most uncomfortable.

"I haven't had time to shop for anything, not even food," he said without apology, stopping suddenly on the way back to the living room, so that she almost collided with him. "What do you think, aside from your insistence that I'm crazy to buy here?"

"It has a lot of possibilities," she admitted reluctantly. "The neighborhood is well cared for and the backyard is huge. But it certainly needs a lot of work. You'll be living in a mess for months, even if you get fast workers in here."

"I thought I'd do most of it myself. Paint, lay some tile in the kitchen and bathroom. Install new fixtures."

"What about your next book?"

"I told you, each one is harder to start. I need to feel right about an idea before actually writing anything. A little manual labor will start my creative juices flowing. It doesn't matter if I don't write anything for a while."

"You're content to rest on your laurels?"

"No, but I don't need money yet. No alimony, just your average crippling settlement, but that was before I signed the contract for *The Farewell Rock.*"

She frowned and walked to the roughhewn fireplace, admiring a triangular rock cleverly cemented between three others. The surface was gritty under her hand, sparkling with minute bits of quartz.

"Just the mention of my book makes you uncomfortable. I think we're going to have to talk about this quite a bit, Hessie—Hester."

"I don't really mind when you call me Hessie," she admitted dejectedly, pressing her forehead against the rough stone.

He touched her hair, falling in fiery ripples on the back of

102

her bright green sweater. She'd taken out the pins that held it in a sleek, dignified halo during the working day.

"Do you mind this?" He reached under the hair and massaged her neck with firmly kneading fingers.

"Actually, I like it," she admitted hoarsely. "It's relaxing."

"Is this relaxing too?"

He pulled her around into his arms, teasingly nibbling at her lips, then rubbing noses with exaggerated playfulness. She would've resisted a passionate kiss, but this made her giggle.

"Do that more often," he said, sliding his hands over her hips, kissing her more vigorously.

"Do what?"

"Giggle, smile, laugh: take your choice."

"I'm not a giddy girl."

He had a genius for reminding her that they couldn't be carefree together.

"I wouldn't want you to be."

Suddenly the game was over. He pressed against her, burying both hands in the fall of hair on her shoulders and crushing her mouth against his. It was happening again, and she was completely sober. She'd come to satisfy her curiosity about his new house, not to expose herself to the spellbinding attraction Adam held for her. All she had to do was say no, walk to the door, and insist he take her home, but his arms were too inviting, his kisses too pleasurable.

He was wearing a velour top, midnight blue with knit cuffs and waistband. The cloth was sensuous to her touch, velvety over his hard shoulders and broad back. She loved stroking it, feeling the nap of the cloth ripple over the muscles underneath.

Inhaling the jasmine fragrance of her hair, he pressed her cheek to his, sighing deeply as a stray tendril tickled his nose.

"I could hold you like this all night."

"I don't think so."

They couldn't be any closer, but Hester felt more cherished than aroused, content for the moment as she rarely had been since Adam had come into her life. Constance was right: sometimes it was awfully nice to have a big strong man to lean on.

Adam kissed her face, trailing his lips from closed lids to the tip of her chin, making her feel meltingly warm when he reached her throat and traced a shivery little path with his tongue.

"I'm becoming obsessed with you," he said softly, sheltering her between his arms. "Before I only loved you; now you've colored my whole world, given it a new brilliance."

"Beautiful words." She hid her face against his shoulder, willing the wet drops in her eyes to dry.

"I can't begin to describe how beautiful you are to me." He sounded humble and a little sad.

But he had described her, endlessly, exactingly, capturing on paper everything from the way she pursed her lips when she was displeased to her habit of counting off her fingers on the pad of her thumb when she was especially bored. Adam made her aware of things in herself that she'd never consciously considered, but he wasn't a comfortable man to love.

"Did you mention something about food?" She pulled away, walking to the front windows, which offered only a view of the drab interior of the porch. "Scraping all that blistered paint will be quite a job."

"I have taken on a monumental task here," he said, not hiding his disappointment, not pretending he meant the renovation of the house.

He walked to a stack of boxes where they'd laid their coats, holding hers until she slipped her arms into it.

"Not all redheads have enough nerve to wear bright yellow."

She frowned.

"It was a compliment. I like it on you."

They ordered dinner for two at a Chinese restaurant, egg rolls, wonton soup, and three platters covered with metal domes to keep the entrees hot: pepper steak, sweet and sour pork, and shrimp fried rice. Eating too much and talking little, she made Adam keep the conversation going. He talked about his parents, his father a museum curator and his mother a counselor at a center for battered women. Like Hester, he was an only child, but he'd grown up in close contact with a boisterous assortment of cousins near his own age. When Hester remained quiet, he threw out ideas for redecorating his house, receiving so little response that he fell silent too.

"Can I come in?" he asked, standing outside her apartment door, hatless as usual and gloveless because he'd left them in the car. "Just to talk."

"There's nothing to say that couldn't have been said at dinner," she said unhappily.

"You did your best to say nothing all evening. I was going to ask you to live with me. I've changed my mind." He sounded petulant.

"That's good. That you've changed your mind. I'm comfortable here. You can see that."

She wasn't talking about her apartment; she wanted him to know that her life was perfectly satisfactory the way it was.

" 'Comfortable.' That's an odd choice of words. Give a fat tabby a bowl of milk and a soft cushion, and you have a comfortable cat. Snug, safe, self-satisfied. What does that have to do with really living?"

"If you're going to be philosophical, I'll pass, Adam." She put her key into the lock. "I have some work to do, and—"

He covered her gloved hand on the knob, pushing the door inward and stepping into the room with her. His surge of anger caught her by surprise, and he'd slammed the door and swept her into his arms before she could react. All his fury went into his kiss, bombarding her mouth as he backed her to the couch. He stopped there, forcing her down on his lap, pummeling her mouth with his.

"You're as hungry for me as I am for you, Hessie. Why make it so complicated?" His voice was an angry growl laced with impatience.

His nylon winterwear was slippery against hers, and she yanked free of his arms, sliding to the floor with a hard thump on her rear. Helpless on her back for an instant, she was pinned by the full weight of his body before she could escape, battling in earnest now, angry at the indignity of grappling on the floor and determined to thwart Adam.

Fiercely pounding on his well-padded back with clenched fists, she fought him, oblivious to the flicker of amusement in his eyes. When she tried to kick, he locked down her legs by straddling them, silencing her with rough kisses. Finally, when one of her blows reddened his ear, he pinned her arms above her head, fending off her attack but not her anger.

"You have no right . . ." she sputtered.

"You do have a temper! I knew no redhead could be as calm and composed as you pretend to be."

"Any woman would fight when she'd been attacked."

"You haven't been attacked!"

His light laughter added more fuel to her anger, and she tried again to struggle free, succeeding only in making him tighten his hold.

"Let me go."

"If you're through fighting me."

"I'm through with you, period! I never want to see you again! Never!"

"You know that's not going to happen. Admit it's not what you really want."

"It is! You're crushing me." She fought for breath, although there was no weight on her lungs.

"Darling, you're going to feel terribly ridiculous in the morning."

"I'm not! I'm not the one who bought a little pink love nest that hasn't been redecorated since the Great Depression."

"It has a new roof and the furnace is good," he said, taunting her with his self-control.

"Let me up." She gritted her teeth together, hating his smile.

"If you're through fighting me."

"I'm not if you touch me with even one finger." She hoped this didn't sound as silly to him as it did to her.

"I've learned my lesson."

His grin was maddening!

She refused his offer of help, trying to scamper up and retain some shred of dignity. Never before had she wrestled on the floor, not even as a toddler! She didn't need to wait until morning to feel ridiculous.

So hot she felt like fainting, she tried to unzip her coat, succeeding only in catching a bit of cloth in the teeth of the zipper. The harder she pulled on the tab, the more firmly the zipper stuck.

"Let me help you."

Backing away, she angrily refused his offer.

"You know, you'll end up cutting yourself free and ruining the coat, so don't be so damn stubborn." His humor seemed to have expended itself. "Hold still and I'll fix it."

"No."

He totally ignored her, coming close and gambling that she'd lost her taste for rough-and-tumble fighting. Her cheeks flamed with crimson while he deftly freed the jammed zipper.

"Have you humiliated me enough?" she asked, hoarse with hostility.

"That's not my intention." He sounded grim. "Just the opposite. We're wasting so much time, Hester. Three years and counting."

"You're wasting your own time. I have things worked out just the way I want them."

"The spinster professor?"

"I've never met your mother, but I can't believe you learned that attitude from her."

"My mother is a warm, giving person, and I don't have an attitude problem. You're my only problem. What do I have to do to break through that shell of yours?"

"I didn't have a shell until you exposed our relationship in your book."

"I wrote about feelings that were important to me. It's called honesty. If you're offended, I'm sorry. I meant it as a memorial to our love, because I was afraid I'd never see you again. If that's all bad, I don't understand your values, Hester."

He left, silently closing the door.

Should she crumple, collapse, cry? Too drained to think, she sank down on the couch still wearing her unzipped coat. What had she done to make a chaotic jumble out of her pleasant, orderly life? She didn't want to be in love with the man who'd betrayed her.

Morning came. Surprisingly she'd slept, but waking up was an ordeal. Just beyond the bedroom door was the room where she'd fought with Adam, writhing on the floor like a woman possessed. How had it happened? With increasing agony, she remembered everything. She knew Adam well; if she'd remained cool, not responding to his unwanted kisses, he would've stopped. But his kisses were never unwanted, and she'd made an absolute fool of herself. She couldn't ever face him again; she couldn't even face herself. Rational, controlled, dignified: none of these words applied to her anymore. Where could she go from here? She must never, never see Adam again, even if it meant living on the other side of the world. This time she'd disappear for good; Adam would never find her. Maybe he'd never bother to look.

In high school she'd been a flag carrier for the band, towering over shorter girls on both sides, marching ahead of the musicians. It was an honor she thoroughly enjoyed, bracing the pole on her body with shoulders back and chin up, loving the dignity of it as the wind whipped the flag above her head. Even before her glorious flag-carrying days, she'd learned to prize composure, to settle arguments with words, to stay cool when others were losing their tempers. Maybe if she'd grown up with a brother in a home where rough-and-tumble combat was a form of fun, she wouldn't feel so devastated by her skirmish with Adam.

He enjoyed it! He wanted her to fight with him on a physical level, goading her to react physically, knowing he could easily win without hurting her. When she struck out at him, she shattered all her own illusions about herself. Instead of a queen, she was a lusty wench battling with a suitor. What could be more devastating than discovering she didn't really know herself?

Tempted to hide from the world, she considered feigning

illness, deciding against it only because missing her classes could bring unwanted attention. Bob Solaski would have to arrange for someone to cover her classes, and friends were sure to call or drop in, expecting her to be really sick, since she'd never taken a day off for illness since coming to Halsted. It was less complicated to go to work and pretend her world wasn't topsy-turvy.

Routine held her together while she plotted an escape. She had to have a job, preferably in her field, but being up for tenure complicated everything. If she applied at another college, they'd assume she was being passed over. No one voluntarily left a position just before the probationary period ended. She might as well brand a big F for failure on her forehead if she didn't wait for the final word on her tenure before job hunting.

Two days passed without word from Adam; it was what she wanted, she told herself. Facing him again would be embarrassing and pointless. Someday she'd look back on this episode in her life and laugh; someday she'd even be able to think about him without a sharp stab of longing.

In the seesaw way that life sometimes treats people, her teaching took a definite upswing. A freshman Russ had sent to her for special help wrote a really tremendous paper, earning an A. Tammy Philips had some great ideas for developing her term paper on women novelists, narrowing the topic and focusing on their relationships with their fathers. She consulted with Hester several times, and the two were becoming friends as well as teacher and student. Tammy wanted to begin her master's right after graduation, and Hester was glad to suggest ways to do it.

Even in the classroom things perked up. A sluggish boy in a morning freshman class came alive when she tapped his hidden talent for dramatic reading. Her least promising class became excited about writing short stories, so she changed her plans to develop this interest. She was feeling more and more like a teacher.

"I'm a darn good teacher!" She laid down her fork and pushed aside the remainder of her luncheon salad, almost defying Constance to contradict her.

109

"I never doubted it," her friend said with mild surprise.

Hester laughed self-consciously. "I didn't mean it quite the way it sounded. My classes have just been picking up a bit and—"

"Don't explain! I know the feeling. For weeks you think you're lecturing to department store window dummies, and suddenly a few seeds take root and sprout. Some of those kids have been listening to you! It's what keeps the good teachers in the classroom."

"What about you?" Hester asked. "Are you still thinking about taking that part in the play?"

"Constantly! But I'm not any closer to making a decision."

"I'd really miss you," Hester said, "but it's exciting to have a choice like that."

What choices did she have? At Halsted she had a good job doing work she loved. Her chances for tenure were excellent; she knew this to be true because Bob Solaski was so cordial. He was notorious for avoiding instructors who were going to be passed over. Her apartment was comfortable and reasonably priced for a college town. She counted many of the faculty members as friends. Just because Adam had installed himself in that dingy pink monstrosity across the river didn't mean she had to sacrifice her career. In the crowded teaching profession, her chances of finding another job weren't good. The cold Wisconsin winters suited her, the university had accepted her for advanced work, and in the summer the beautiful beaches of Lake Michigan were invitingly close.

"Exciting, but nerve-racking," Constance said. "I have an appointment in seven minutes. I'll see you later."

Deciding to stay no matter what Adam did, Hester felt a little better about herself. There would never be another humiliating scene between them, and if he wrote about anything that had happened, she'd sue. In fact, it seemed like a good idea to warn him ahead of time to leave her out of all of his future novels.

Screwing up her courage, she decided to call and tell him exactly that as soon as she returned to her apartment after classes.

Calling information, she was given his phone number, further proof that the house wasn't just an elaborate practical joke.

"Hello." His voice sounded warm and expectant.

"Adam, it's Hester."

"I wondered when you'd call, love."

His breezy tone was irritating beyond words.

"There's no reason in the world for you to expect a call from me!"

"But you have called, haven't you?"

"There's no reason to be smug! This is a business call!"

"Do we have business dealings?"

"Yes, serious ones. I've been thinking about *The Farewell Rock*, and I don't want you to write another word about me, ever."

"I create fictional characters," he said slowly. "If I borrow from real life, it's at least partially subconscious."

"You're twisting things. You can't deny using me in your last book."

"I'm not trying to deny it, but I won't apologize for writing about the woman I love."

"Well, don't do it anymore!"

"Love you?"

"Write about me!"

"But it's okay to love you?"

"No, it's not! But I called to talk about your next book and your next and all the rest."

"You don't want to be in them?"

"Absolutely not!"

"So if I have my hero and heroine wrestle on the floor, you'll jump to the conclusion that I'm writing about us?"

Her cheeks turned hot pink, even though there was no one there to see.

"I'm talking about anything you borrow from real life."

"And how do you propose to monitor my writing? Should I send you daily copies or will once a week be often enough?"

"I never want to read another word you write." She was losing control of the conversation and hated herself for it.

"If you do use me, I'll sue, Adam. I swear I'll get a lawyer and take you to court."

"The publicity would sell a ton of books. How will you know whether to sue if you don't read another word I write?"

"I can tell just by skimming the book!"

"I've accused a couple of reviewers of doing that, but I expected better from you."

"This conversation is getting us nowhere."

"At least I know you still care," he said dryly.

"Care!"

"Enough to yell at me."

"I'm not yelling! Good—"

"Wait, don't hang up."

"I don't want to argue."

"Then have dinner with me."

"No, I don't think so."

"Anyplace you say. I'll even cook for you."

"No."

"This weekend, then. We'll go to Chicago and stay at the—"

"Adam, no!"

"Separate rooms?" he suggested meekly.

"No rooms at all."

"Well, call me tomorrow. I'll come up with a better idea."

"I'm not—"

"Okay, okay, I'll call you."

"You interrupted me!"

"Haven't you said no enough times for one evening?"

"Apparently not!" She lowered her voice, afraid she'd been shouting.

"I'll call you. Think about it."

He hung up first, much to her annoyance.

She wasn't going to think about a call from him tomorrow. In fact, she spent the whole next day thinking about not thinking about his call. By five o'clock she dreaded going home, but what was there for a single woman to do on a Friday night in Vienne, Wisconsin?

Hester enjoyed entertaining; maybe she could get a four-

112

some together for bridge the next evening or invite a few friends for a casual buffet. Her beef stroganoff was quick to prepare, if she had the butcher cut the meat. In fact, she owed the Solaskis a dinner, and they enjoyed bridge. Professor Hughes in the history department, a widower close to retirement, loved the game and would make an ideal fourth. She put her plan into action the minute she got home, not wanting time for second thoughts.

"Julie," she said when Mrs. Solaski answered the phone. "This is Hester Paine. I've been dying to play some bridge. I wondered if the two of you could come for dinner tomorrow, and I'll ask a fourth so we can play a few rubbers."

"We'd love to. Let me check the calendar here." After a pause she asked, "Have you asked anyone else yet, Hester?"

"No, you're the first one I called."

"I have a tiny problem. Bob wrote on the calendar: 'Dinner here, Adam S-W.' I remember him asking me about it last week, but this will work out perfectly. You can come here instead, and we'll have a foursome."

"Oh, I couldn't do that!" She thought frantically for a plausible excuse. "I'd be intruding."

"Nonsense! Oh, here's Bob now. I'll make sure he didn't have any other plans for the evening."

"Julie . . ."

The thud of the receiver landing on the counter was followed by dead silence. Hester prayed that Bob Solaski had three tickets for something or some other reason to veto his wife's suggestion.

"Hester"—Bob spoke into the phone himself—"great idea. I was wondering what we'd do to entertain a famous author."

"Maybe he doesn't play bridge," Hester suggested desperately.

"Then we'll play Monopoly. Here's Julie. She'll give you the details."

"Just dress casually, Hester. Be here around six, so we'll have lots of time to play."

"I really wanted to cook a dinner for you," Hester said. "You haven't been here since before Christmas."

"I love to cook. Tell you what, you can whip up a dessert. Something not too fattening. I always do too much taste-testing when I bake. We'll see you tomorrow."

The phone rang at half-hour intervals throughout the evening, but she didn't even consider answering it. The infernal instrument had gotten her in enough trouble for one night. Adam would think she wanted to spend the evening with him tomorrow.

Julie had said casual; Hester preferred austere. She dressed for the evening in a gray wool pantsuit that fit well but was out of style and drab. Usually she wore a bright-colored top with it, but the black man-tailored blouse she chose tonight better matched her mood. Let Adam see that her being there wasn't her idea of a party. She certainly wasn't going for the pleasure of his company.

His car was in the Solaskis' driveway when she arrived. She parked behind it, not worrying about blocking him. The evening couldn't end too soon to suit her; she certainly would be the first to leave, even if she had to invent a headache. The pie she'd thrown together using a preprepared graham cracker crust and cherry filling from a can wasn't a very impressive dessert to be offering to her boss's wife, but there was enough whipped cream on it to hide her shortcomings as a cook, at least until they were all stuffed from Julie's expert cooking.

"Hester, you've met Adam. I was so sorry to miss meeting him myself at the dean's party," Julie said, ushering her into a large living room that managed to look crowded in spite of the ample floor space.

The Solaskis loved heavy furniture. The three-piece davenport, love seat, and chair set had massive arms and thick cushions upholstered in a whimsical blue and gold floral pattern, the occasional tables had legs like oak trunks, and the television cabinet was five hundred pounds of walnut surrounding a large screen. Julie matched her furniture, stout and solid. Her husband was lean except for a desk worker's pot belly. Hester often felt fortunate that he headed the English department, but tonight was the exception.

She'd be safer with the dean, who rationed out his invitations strictly on the basis of status.

"Hester, nice to see you." Adam stood to greet her, taking her cold fingers in his warm hand.

"Bob, stir up the fire and throw on another log. I have to check the roast." Julie never languished in her husband's shadow.

"Let me help," Hester offered urgently.

"No need. Everything's under control. Should I put your pie in the fridge?"

"Please. It's nothing spectacular, I'm afraid. Let me take the foil off the top."

"No, no, you just keep the men occupied while I get things on the table."

Where were the weak little women like Mrs. Williamson when she needed one?

"Adam's bought a house," Bob said. "It looks like our humble town has a resident novelist."

"How nice," Hester said, meeting Adam's gaze as the English professor tended his fireplace.

"My writing's on hold while I do some redecorating," Adam said.

"Do you have an idea for your next novel?" she asked, a question interesting enough to distract Bob from his fire.

"Only a germ of an idea."

"Using a campus setting?" she pressed.

"Possibly. I never talk about my ideas before I work them out. Maybe because they sound too silly when they're underdeveloped."

"I know just what you mean," Solaski said. "A novel's private. I've been working on one for six years, and not even my wife has read any of it."

"Oh, you're a writer?" Adam asked politely.

"Like all English profs, I have the great American novel stewing on a back burner. I dread retirement; no more excuses not to work on it."

"And you, Hester," Adam asked, "are you going to write a book someday?"

"Not fiction. Literary criticism is more my field."

"I'll have to show you a galley of my next novel. Let you scoop the literary world with a review in the *Vienne Herald.*"

"It's a good idea to publish, Hester," her boss reminded her. "Counts a lot when you're considered for advancement."

"Why not review *The Farewell Rock?*" Adam suggested, refusing to let the subject lie.

"I'm sure the campus paper would print it," Bob said.

"Maybe Julie can use some help," she said evasively.

"Oh, no, let me warn you. When my wife cooks, I'm afraid to go into the kitchen for a beer. That's her territory. But fortunately I keep my liquor cabinet in here. What would you like, Hester?"

"Chablis," Adam answered for her.

"Sherry, if you have it," she contradicted, noticing their host's puzzled frown.

Dinner was delicious. Julie's crown rack of veal was a masterpiece, served with a crisp salad, sauteed vegetables, and cheese bread. It was the kind of meal that satisfied completely without stuffing. Hester was quick to suggest they save her pie for later. No one helped do anything in Julie Solaski's kitchen, she discovered, thrown for a second time into the company of the men. She escaped temporarily to renew her lipstick.

"Well, Adam, how about the men taking on the women?" Bob asked, setting up the card table for bridge.

"Fine with me." He ran his eyes lazily over Hester in a look so frankly sensual that she blushed. Julie came into the room with homemade brandied chocolates to put on the table.

Julie liked to chat while she played, but it was Adam who spoiled Hester's playing. She couldn't compress her legs enough to avoid the brush of his calf or the bump of his knee, little gestures that continually reminded her that he was more than a bridge opponent. Once, when his ankle found hers, she wanted to tell him to stop playing kids' games. The way he was making her feel had nothing to do with bridge.

The women lost badly, hardly surprising since Julie never counted trump and Hester was flustered by Adam's veiled innuendos. Bob was the only person concentrating on bridge. The evening seemed endless to Hester, but it was finally climaxed by the serving of her pie, which fell apart coming out of the foil pan. They ate messy heaps of cherries and whipped cream and called it an evening.

Practically running to her car, Hester managed to avoid any personal conversation with Adam, but he pulled out of the drive immediately after she did, the lights of his New Yorker staying close all the way to her apartment. She parked in back, hoping he hadn't stopped.

"I had a nice evening." He was lounging beside her door by the time she had walked around to the front.

"I couldn't get out of going to their house," she said.

"This has got to stop, you know."

"Let me open my door, please."

He stepped aside, watching her fumble for the keyhole.

"It's late, Adam. I'm tired."

"I won't keep you from bed."

"No more."

"No more what?" he asked.

"Verbal fencing. You win. You're much more clever than I am. I'm no match for you, so just leave me alone."

"I'm still a little worried about being sued."

"I'm not suing. I never will, if you leave me out of your novels."

"You'll see yourself in every book, if you want to."

"Next you'll be telling me I wasn't in *The Farewell Rock.*"

"No, I'll never say that."

"I'm going in. Good night, Adam."

"I'd like to be invited inside. I won't force myself on you." He sounded terribly unhappy.

"Adam." She felt weary and exasperated, wanting him to come in more than she'd admit to herself. "All right. Just for coffee."

"I promise to leave the minute you ask."

He was quiet, abnormally so, laying his storm coat over

117

the back of a chair and sitting on the couch while she fixed instant coffee for him.

"Aren't you having anything?" he asked, accepting the cup.

"No." Her throat had seemed unaccountably dry, so she'd had a glass of water in the kitchen.

When she sat on a chair to his right, he didn't comment, only watching her with a puzzling expression.

"How's your house coming?" she asked, to break the awkward silence.

"Slowly. There was dry rot in some of the kitchen floorboards. I've had a carpenter helping me all week."

"Is it really worth the trouble, Adam?"

"To me it is." He sipped his coffee.

"Well, have you decided what color to paint the outside?"

"Does the pink make you uncomfortable?" he asked.

"It doesn't matter to me one way or the other!"

She stood and paced, on the verge of asking him to leave, even though he was the most exciting man she'd ever met. With his legs crossed she could see the muscles of his thighs bulging against the navy wool of his slacks, and the white cable-knit sweater he was wearing called attention to broad shoulders and chest. She wanted to be held, petted, and sheltered, yearnings that were making her feel girlish and vulnerable.

He stood with an effortless motion, walking toward the kitchen with his cup.

"I'll have to teach you how to make coffee," he said with a casual, proprietary air.

"I'd appreciate it if you'd go now, Adam."

"I promised I would, and I will," he said in a noncommittal voice.

She picked up his coat, only intending to hand it to him, surprised when he turned his back to her, expecting her to help him with it.

"You want me to hold your coat for you?" She straightened it and made the gesture.

"Thank you. And thanks for the coffee."

He turned, so close that he filled her vision, but left his coat open, the belt hanging loose on either side.

"We're still wasting time, darling," he said so softly she just managed to hear.

Like a moth attracted to a fire, she leaned forward, caught in his arms as his lips came down on hers.

What's a kiss? she thought solemnly, her last conscious thought for many minutes. Adam was sucking her mouth, creating the most incredible sensation, making her tingle with desire. She forgot to say no as he inflicted a sweeter torture than any she'd ever imagined, inflaming her senses in a chain reaction that made her ache for him.

His hands rested on her shoulders, kneading and stroking, moving to the back of her neck and upward to loosen her hair. When it fell to her shoulders, he took one strand and brought it to his cheek.

"We're losing so much time," he whispered hoarsely, stepping away from her.

Reaching toward him with one hand, she stared into eyes half clouded with passion.

"Good night, Hessie."

He stepped around her as if nothing at all had happened, leaving before she could react.

She went to her knees on the floor on the spot where he'd left her, shaking with a need so strong she cried aloud. Stricken, her whole body clenched into a knot of misery, she felt a terrible loss but didn't understand it. Physical yearning was part of it, a painful part, but there was more, a hollowness, an insufficiency. She craved Adam but didn't want to need him. For years she'd been putting her personality together, assembling it like pieces of a jigsaw puzzle. Now with one convulsive upheaval, the pieces were all jumbled together. She didn't know how to go back and redo it, and going ahead without Adam was unbearable.

She cried there on the floor, letting a torrent of tears wash unchecked over her face, shivering from shock and longing. Adam was destroying her. Her love for him was dangerous and consuming. She didn't know who she was anymore.

CHAPTER SEVEN

Time healed, her mother always said, and Hester wanted to believe it. All she had to do was be more wary of issuing and accepting invitations, and weeks might pass without seeing Adam. The town was big enough for both of them, she hoped.

Wednesday was her least favorite day. The mailman delivered nothing but bills and occupant fliers, students came to class with excuses instead of reading the assignments, and Professor Solaski conducted his twice-monthly departmental meetings. This week it was going to be a long one. Brad had a ninety-seven-page survey of collective bargaining on the college level; he hoped it would prod the English department into taking the lead in organizing the faculty.

The meeting went as Hester expected. Brad argued with the department head for seventeen minutes before Solaski grudgingly gave him five minutes to present a condensed version of his report. Brad took twenty-one minutes, then complained that he'd gotten much better response from the paper technology department. Hester envied their resident poet; she'd brought her knitting, busily clicking the needles through the two-hour-and-eleven-minute meeting.

"Hester, can I see you for a minute?" Bob Solaski asked as his few department members rose stiffly from the hard oak chairs in his roomy but antiquated office.

It was too soon to hear about her tenure, but she stood waiting as apprehensively as a child being kept after school.

"I have a surprise for you," he said when they were alone. "Adam Smith-Woodham has volunteered to do some guest lectures. He'll do them without compensation just to get the feel of the campus for his next book."

"How nice." Again she was being a hypocrite, hating herself for not speaking her mind.

"Princely," her boss said, beaming. "With our budget, we couldn't afford five minutes of his time. Naturally I thought of your modern-novel class."

"My class? Wouldn't that be a waste of his talent to speak to such a small group?"

"No, he specifically requested a classroom situation instead of a special lecture."

"He's going to take over my class?" A sick churning in the pit of her stomach made her sit down.

"Nothing like that! You'll still be totally responsible for all papers, grading, and such. What he suggested is a series of six lectures spread out over a three-week period. Let's see, that class meets on Monday, Wednesday, and Friday. Give him the next three Mondays and Wednesdays; you can use Fridays to sum up."

"I have my plans made for the rest of the semester. The class is reading—"

"How many kids in a small college like this have a chance to hear one of today's leading novelists? Their children may study his books as assigned reading some day."

He spoke with unusual gruffness that discouraged her from further argument. She nodded with a meekness she didn't feel.

"Give him a call at this number to confirm the days, would you please?" He handed her a blue memo slip. "The four of us will have to get together for bridge again soon."

Fortunately he was in a hurry to leave and didn't notice her expression.

Adam had gone too far this time! She stormed out to her car, infuriated at the audacity of the man. He was supersensitive when she criticized his book. Didn't he realize that her

121

work was important too? Teaching a class on the novel was the highlight of her year. Giving six class periods to him meant that all her plans were ruined. She'd have to scrap carefully prepared lectures, shorten the assigned reading list, and write a new exam with midterms only weeks away. Adam would entertain her class, but he'd also cause havoc with her well-organized course.

Too angry for a telephone confrontation, she drove to his ugly pink house. He came to the door wearing paint-speckled old jeans and an equally spattered plaid shirt hanging loose over his waist. The smell of fresh paint was strong, and the living room was a confused jumble of drop cloths, ladders, and still unopened boxes. A burly-looking man in overalls was rolling ivory paint on a far wall.

"Hester, come in, but be careful not to touch anything. I'd hate to see you get paint on your coat."

"I thought you'd be alone."

"Harry," he said, raising his voice. "This is Hester Paine, a friend of mine from the college. Hester, Harry McMaster. I finally got tired of this mess and brought in a pro to help me. By next week we should have the inside done."

Hester acknowledged the painter with a stiff smile. He nodded and kept on painting.

"I need to talk to you alone," she whispered.

"We're going to send out for pizza and work until this room is finished. It's taking three coats to cover the old oil paint. Want to join us? Painting or pizza, take your choice. You'd look good in a pair of my old jeans."

"I'm not here to help you redecorate this folly," she said, angry to the bursting point.

"A private talk?"

"Please."

"Come out to the kitchen."

She didn't want to admit how pleasant the old room was. The cupboards had been painted a plum-red to match the fanciful knives, forks, and spoons dancing on white wallpaper. Gleaming new buff-colored tiles lightened the room even more, and with the dingy curtains gone, the window revealed the snow-swept panorama of the backyard with apple trees and leafless lilac bushes. In the spring it would be lovely.

"Like it?" he asked casually.

"Very nice."

"But you're not here on a tour of inspection?"

"Why did you do it, Adam?"

"Do what?"

"Take over my class."

"Six lectures is hardly taking over. I thought I'd help you. Solaski was impressed that we're old friends. Your tenure is a sure thing."

"You can't know that."

"I asked."

"Oh, no!"

"I didn't want to go through with all this redecorating and have you leave town."

"I can't believe it! You've moved into my life, and I have nothing to say about it!"

"You have everything to say," he said softly, wiping his hands on a sheaf of paper toweling and looking thoughtfully at the smears of paint.

Too exasperated for the moment to say more about the class, she said, "There's paint under your eye. You look like a clown."

"My paint spatters are your protection. I'm too much of a gentleman to kiss you when I'm a mess."

"My class, Adam. Please tell Solaski you've changed your mind."

"When will I see you again?"

"You won't! Can't you see that we should go our separate ways?"

"I'm crazy not to. You hurt me when you disappeared, Hessie. I've never needed anyone more."

"There was no way I could know you really wanted me."

"Darling, I told you every way I knew how."

"Your letters said you loved me, but you stayed away so long!"

"Only because I had to!" He took her hand, then dropped

123

it, remembering the dots of paint on his arm that had splattered from the roller.

"It's not working, Adam. I don't want to catch you on the rebound. . . ."

"That's crazy after all this time! I loved you before my divorce and I love you now. You're inventing difficulties that don't exist!"

She wanted to tell him that the pain of missing him, the hurt of realizing he might never leave his wife, wasn't imaginary, but instead she bit her lip. He'd managed to rekindle feelings so volatile that she was suffering from emotional exhaustion, and only his interference in her work seemed a safe subject to argue about.

"Let me tell you . . ." he said.

"Please don't! Just call Bob Solaski and tell him you won't be able to lecture. Say your new book demands your whole attention."

"I haven't started one."

"Marvelous use of your time, being a painter's helper."

"It gives me a lot of time to think."

"You're avoiding my question. Will you please stay away from my class?"

"Are you afraid of competition?"

"Of course not!"

"Then what harm will my lectures do?"

"I have the rest of the semester planned: readings, lectures, exams. Everything will be thrown out of kilter if I lose six class periods."

"Give me your lesson plans, and I'll gear my lectures to them. Solaski will be pleased, and your class will get some practical insight into writing a book."

"They're reading them, not writing them," she said, losing her last traces of patience.

"You're afraid to compete with me." He wiped his hands on the sides of his jeans, getting a fresh smear of paint on his fingers.

"No, that's not it at all!"

"Isn't it? You won't mind if I contradict things you've

124

already told your class? You won't feel threatened if my views don't coincide with yours?"

"That's not fair, Adam!"

"Maybe not, but I still think you're afraid of me."

"That's preposterous!"

"Preposterous. Good word, but a little dated. I don't think I've used it in any of my books."

"I wish I'd never met you!"

"Knowing you hasn't exactly made my life a bed of roses either."

"Then why don't you leave me alone? There's no reason for you to live here."

"There is now. Even pink stucco bungalows are expensive these days."

"I can't stand this!" She headed for the door, sidestepping an opened paint can and a cluster of boxes.

Following close behind, he reached the car just after she did.

"What days?" he asked, standing beside a gritty-looking pile of snow in shirt sleeves.

"It's too cold to be out without a coat."

"See, you're always concerned about my welfare. Doesn't that tell something about how much you love me?" He wasn't faking a shiver.

"Oh . . ."

"I can start next week."

"I'm sure you don't have to bother preparing your lectures."

"I do, but I can use a series I gave a few years ago."

"Convenient. My orders were to give you Monday and Wednesday for three weeks running."

"Can we talk about the class ahead of time? That way I won't step on your toes, and you can plan more easily."

"I'll see you in class, not before."

"If that's what you want." He closed the car door for her, watching in spite of the cold while she backed out of the drive.

She prepared her class for his arrival, telling them to eliminate one book from their semester reading list. Not surprisingly, they were enthusiastic. Not only would they hear a famous novelist, their outside work load was lessened. Everyone was delighted about Adam's offer, she thought dejectedly, but each hour he spent there would be an ordeal for her.

He was late. At five minutes after the hour she gave him a deadline; if he didn't come by ten after, she'd dismiss the students. It wasn't her fault if the famous guest lecturer didn't show.

He arrived with a minute to spare, delivering a witty, perceptive talk. Afterward several girls, including Tammy Philips, clustered around him, asking questions and forgetting their other classes. She didn't join the admiring throng.

She'd never claimed psychic powers, but driving home, she felt certain Adam would make an appearance that evening. If he gloated over his smashing success, she'd explode!

Teachers weren't one big happy family; as in any profession, there were rivalries and competition. Each educator was sure that his or her class was the most inspiring and worthwhile. Hester had a good rapport with her students and worked hard to broaden their understanding of the literature she loved. It seemed so unfair that Adam could come to class, entertain them, and walk away a hero without being responsible for the less desirable things like reading papers, preparing exams, and grading. Old Ms. Paine was going to seem awfully dull after a glamorous author staged six performances.

She tried to overcome her resentment, telling herself the students were lucky to hear a well-known novelist. It had never been her style to be petty or jealous. She didn't much like herself now, but Adam had killed her enthusiasm for the class, forcing her to set aside carefully made plans.

Settling for a TV dinner and a wedge of lettuce, she finished the evening meal and turned her attention to some freshman quizzes, glad that the short answers didn't require much concentration.

Adam came at nine thirty, just when she'd relaxed and stopped expecting him.

"Can I come in?"

126

"Don't you mean, May I come in?"

"No, I'm not asking for permission. I want to know if it's safe."

"For you or me?"

"I won't even take my coat off." He stepped into the living room and stood on the plastic mat she used to protect the carpet in winter.

"What do you want?" She was too disheartened to fence with him.

"If you don't want me to lecture in your class, I won't do it anymore. Today will have been my first and last time."

"You were a big hit. Why change your mind now?"

"Hessie, I only have one thing on my mind: you. Everything I do backfires. When I wrote the book, I hoped you'd read it and come back to me. It just never occurred to me that you'd be hurt by it." He unconsciously unbuttoned his storm coat, warm in the overcharged atmosphere.

She wanted to hug him, to hold him in her arms and make everything right between them, but she didn't know how to take that step.

"You were talking about my class."

"Fast learners. They were really enthusiastic. You've done a good job with them."

"They'll learn a lot from you."

"They're already learning plenty from you. I'll think of an excuse to give Solaski."

"It's too late, Adam."

"In what way?"

"I've already announced that you'll give six lectures. I canceled part of their reading assignment. The class wouldn't be thrilled to have it reassigned. The schedule is already hopelessly upset, you see."

He'd offer to quit, and she was persuading him not to. Sometimes she couldn't understand herself.

"Hessie, if you don't want me lecturing to your class . . ."

"It's all arranged." She shrugged her shoulders, wishing he wouldn't watch her so closely.

"I've lectured a lot, but I've never taught. I guess there's a difference."

"A big one," she agreed.

"You know why I did it."

"Why you offered to lecture?"

"It was just another excuse to see you. We're still wasting minutes, hours, days, Hessie."

"My time isn't wasted."

"You can plan your time wisely but not your life."

"More philosophy?"

He was standing very close, still wearing the heavy fur-collared coat. When he stroked her cheek with the backs of his fingers, she felt a great tenderness for him.

"I have a proposal," he said softly.

"No, Adam . . ."

"Just hear me out. We'll start from scratch, just the way I suggested in the motel at Madison. Friends first. An occasional dinner, maybe a movie or a concert. Nothing heavy, I promise. We'll get reacquainted."

"It wouldn't stay that way," she said unhappily.

"It's worth trying. I'm running out of schemes to see you."

"Like lecturing to my class?"

"My ideas aren't getting any better, I admit. No wonder I can't get started on a new book."

"You're researching Halsted College."

"I'm not very proud of that excuse for being here. Maybe I'll have to write a book just to look honest. I'm hot. Can I take my coat off?"

"You may."

"That's why you're the teacher. My editor corrects my grammar."

"How helpful."

"Slowly, we'll go slowly," he said, laying the heavy coat over the desk chair.

"You're not going to give up, are you?"

"No, and I don't think you want me to."

Struggling to be honest with herself, she just wasn't sure. If he kissed her now, she'd want more, but she wasn't comfortable with him. It wasn't just aging cats who needed a soft cushion in life. Adam was too unpredictable.

"I just don't know, Adam."

"There's no one else?"

"No."

"You plan to continue teaching?"

"Yes."

"Then time is on my side."

"Or mine," she said so softly, he asked her to repeat it. She didn't.

"We could start by taking a walk."

"I'd like to do that."

He helped with her wool coat, turning up the collar around her neck because her hair was still pinned up in the usual working-day style.

"Do you think the zero days are over?" he asked.

"I hope so, but we could still get some snowstorms."

"Before I saw you again, I was thinking of getting a house somewhere in the Southwest, maybe Phoenix or San Diego."

"You'd have a coast-to-coast string of cottages."

"The next place I buy will be in perfect condition. Maybe a new condo. I'm such a sloppy painter, I practically have to take a bath in turpentine."

"I've never heard of using turpentine with latex paint."

"I exaggerated. Author's license."

"Have you finished painting?"

"Not quite. Then there's unpacking and buying some furniture. You wouldn't consider helping me pick out a couch and some chairs, would you?"

"No."

"Too cozy?"

"You're setting up housekeeping. I already have a home, and I don't think I should help you."

They walked along semidark streets, the lights overhead glowing pinkly under a star-filled sky. He thrust his hands, gloveless as usual, into deep coat pockets, tucking one of hers into the depths with his. The wind tousled his hair and threatened to loosen hers, but they weren't cold.

Outside her door he took the key and opened it, stepping inside but again stopping on the plastic mat.

"You're sure you want me to finish the lectures?" he asked.

"It's too late to cancel them."

"Anytime you want me to stop, just say so."

"Thank you, Adam."

"For offering to quit?"

"For being nice."

"I'll see you Wednesday, then. Will you have dinner with me that evening?"

"In a restaurant?"

"Yes."

"All right."

"Is a good-night kiss rushing you?"

"I don't think—"

At first he seemed content to brush her lips with his, inhaling the fresh fragrance of her skin. Coming into the warm room after their brisk walk in the cold made her sleepy, and she rested her cheek against his, not resisting when his arms circled her waist.

"I'd like to hold you all night," he murmured.

She pulled away and looked into his face. There was longing in his expression, and love, but he was smiling.

"Another five minutes?" He held open palms toward her.

"Good night, Adam."

After waiting ten minutes for Adam to come on Wednesday, she told the class they could go, but Tammy Philips insisted they wait a few more minutes.

"In one of his books, Mr. Smith-Woodham said, 'The time clock is a ruthless master.' I'm sure he'll be here soon."

Annoyed by his tardiness, Hester wanted to leave herself, but Tammy persuaded all but one rebel to wait for the lecturer. Her faith was rewarded when Adam came into the room nearly twenty minutes late for a class scheduled to last fifty minutes. Hester felt like strangling him!

If his lecture had anything to do with modern novels, she didn't hear that part. He talked about swimming in the ocean, asked the students what they liked about Halsted, and related several escapades from his own undergraduate days. Instead of learning about Hemingway and Steinbeck, her students were hearing jokes recycled from Abbott and Costello.

As soon as she was free for the day, Hester sought out Constance at Sadler Hall.

"Do you have time for a cup of tea?" Hester asked.

"If you don't mind the instant kind I keep in my office. I'm holding auditions for the spring play starting in half an hour."

"Your department is never dull!"

"I have more exciting news than that. Come on."

Constance's office was tucked into the basement of Sadler Hall with ducts for steam pipes crossing the ceiling, but it was roomier and more colorful than Hester's. Reproductions of old theater posters covered the walls, and props from past plays vied for space with an extensive library of plays. The desk was pushed into a corner and seldom used; Constance preferred to operate from a casual grouping of leather-padded chairs around a low, round table. She spooned instant tea into styrofoam cups and added water kept hot all day in an automatic coffee maker.

"You look like you're bursting to tell me something," Hester said, taking a cup and cautiously testing the temperature with a tiny sip.

"Bursting is the word! I did it, Hester!"

"You took the part?"

"I signed and mailed my contract this morning."

"Congratulations! I'm going to miss you, but it's so exciting! Will the company come to Wisconsin?"

"No, not next season, but I'll send you some tickets for Chicago."

"Are you taking a leave of absence?"

"No." She looked grave. "I'm resigning. I'm going to make it, Hester. If I know there's no turning back, I'll have to be a success. I've wanted to be a serious actress since I was ten. It's now or never."

"You'll do it! You have the talent and the ambition."

131

"There aren't many parts out there for a black Barrymore," Constance said wryly, "but I'm going to give it a shot."

"It'll be lonesome here without you."

"If it is, it'll be your own fault. How much longer are you going to pretend you're not in love with Adam Smith-Woodham?"

"You don't know what he's doing now! He talked Solaski into letting him be a guest lecturer in my novel class. He's turning it into a fiasco!"

"He does have your attention, though."

Two could play his game. She visited with Constance until the auditions started, made an unnecessary stop at her office, and managed to arrive home twenty minutes after the time she'd agreed to meet Adam for dinner. He was waiting in his car across the street, the only side where parking was allowed.

"Busy day?" he asked lazily, following her into the apartment.

"Very."

"Where would you like to go for dinner?"

"Anywhere. It doesn't matter."

"Are you angry?"

"No. Would you like a drink while I freshen up?"

"I'll help myself. Is it because I was late? I can tell you're not happy with me. A plumber came just as I was leaving."

"If your renovating is so demanding, why did you offer to lecture to my class?"

"I never mentioned your class to Solaski."

"No, I just happen to teach the only modern-novel class on campus."

They got through dinner by talking about the weather, which was damp and slushy, the dinner, which featured mediocre lamb chops and dry baked potatoes, and politics, one of the few areas where they were in agreement.

"See," he said with a winning grin, "it's not so hard being friends."

"About my class, Adam, I was going to discuss—"

132

"My offer is still open. Give the word and I won't finish my lecture series."

"You're not lecturing! You're entertaining! How can I give an exam on what you're presenting?"

"You want me to be more serious?"

"Oh, Adam, can't—"

"How about a movie?" he interrupted.

"I don't think so. I have a full schedule tomorrow."

"We'll just go to your place, then."

"No," she said quickly. "Maybe a movie would be relaxing."

It had to be more calming than having Adam in her apartment.

"Good."

"But I'll have to call it a night right afterward."

"That's fine with me. Harry is coming at seven to help paint the bathroom."

The theater was so empty, they had a row to themselves with no one near them. Adam helped with her coat, went back for a cardboard bucket of popcorn, and settled down beside her.

The movie starred an actor who always played himself with varying degrees of success, this time chasing an actress young enough to be his daughter. No one in the sparse audience laughed at his antics.

She refused the popcorn, so Adam ate all of it, taking out a handkerchief to wipe away the butter on his fingers. Wishing she hadn't come, Hester sat clutching her purse on her lap, too aware of the man beside her to follow the story on the screen. He reached over and covered her bunched fist with his hand, wiggling his thumb under one clenched finger, patiently stroking until her hand relaxed in his, their fingers interlaced.

There was a car chase on the screen, but it could've been recycled from any one of a dozen other films. Adam released her hand but caressed her knee, slowly inching upward.

"Stop!" she whispered urgently, attempting to dislodge his hand.

"We practically have the theater to ourselves." He leaned over and flicked his tongue into her ear.

He knew what he was doing, subtly assaulting her senses until she forgot the movie on the big screen in front of them. She couldn't leave without being conspicuous, not that she had her own car, but he was taking unfair advantage, working his hand under her skirt to the soft, fleshy part of her thigh.

"Stop or I'm leaving," she hissed.

He did, but she couldn't forget the warmth of his hand audaciously slipping between her legs, making her throb with frustration. Just when she'd willed herself to calmly ignore him, his knee brushed against hers, then his elbow invaded her territory. He was crowding her into continual awareness of him, and she tensed, expecting another invasion by his hand.

He sighed, coughed, shifted in his seat, and whispered something she didn't quite catch. When his arm settled across the back of her seat, she pulled her coat around her shoulders and tried to shrink down. The movie finally ended just as his thumb was making lazy circles on the nape of her neck, sending shivery sensations down her spine.

"I will never go to another movie with you," she stormed when they were out on the street headed toward his car.

"We'll get cable TV. I'd love to make love to you on a bearskin rug while the cavalry rushes out to fight the Indians." He tooted his own version of a bugle charge and pulled her to him with one arm.

"You think it's funny to act like a horny high schooler!"

"No, there's nothing funny about the way I want you. You're driving me crazy, Hessie." He opened the car door for her, then walked around to the driver's side.

"This isn't going to work," she said morosely, "pretending we're just friends out on a date."

"No. Live with me, Hester."

"Adam . . ."

"You can move in next week. Everything will be settled. If necessary, I'll pay off the rest of your lease. I can't write with you on the other side of the river. Every time I face a piece of paper, I want to describe how smooth your skin is and how your hair crackles with electricity when you pull out the pins."

"Stop! Please, Adam!"

"Would it be so terrible to live with me? I'm a passable cook and a terrific lover."

"Modest, too."

"I'm not making any claims you can't substantiate for yourself."

"You've intruded on my personal feelings, my social life, my professional life, my class . . ."

"Intruded? Is that what I've done?"

"You never give me any choice. What else would you call it?"

"I'd call it trying to thaw the coldest woman I've ever met. You're not frigid in bed, Hessie. Why insist on playing the ice maiden?"

"That is such a superficial judgment! You really don't know me at all."

"If I don't, it isn't because I haven't been trying!"

"This is pointless! Take me home!"

"Not yet. I want to hear it all—all the resentments you've been harboring."

"You are so inconsiderate!"

"Because I was late to your class?"

"Because of everything! What if someone saw you lifting up my skirt in a public place?"

"There weren't more than a dozen people dozing through that movie, and I didn't do anything to sully your honor! I've tried everything I know to make you realize you're a woman! Would it be so terrible to lie in my arms every night and come alive just for me?"

"I'm alive enough without your groping and grabbing!"

"Is that what I do? Then what do you call this?"

He leaned over, oblivious to the empty but well-lit street where he'd parked, kissing her with emphatic boldness.

"I wish I could get you out of my system," he said angrily.

"Maybe I'm just a challenge to you after all your easy coed conquests!"

"Coed conquests! I haven't dated a college girl since I was an undergraduate."

"They fawn on you, and you love it!"

He eyed her shrewdly for a moment, then started the car and pulled away from the curb with a skidding sound, the tires sliding on the sand left by city crews through the icy winter.

"You're driving like a teen-ager too!"

"Is there anything about me that you do like?" he demanded.

There were a million things, but she was too angry to tell him that.

"I like it that you're willing to stop your lectures. Please don't come to my class anymore."

"That offer is withdrawn. I have four more sessions, and I'll be there for all of them—on time."

"You said—"

"I've changed my mind. My good friend Bob Solaski expects me to finish the series. He's writing an article about them for the alumni quarterly."

"He would!"

"It wouldn't hurt if you got off your duff and published some articles."

"I'm not the one who's playing handyman instead of working! How many words have you written since coming here?"

"I wrote a letter to my parents and signed some valentines," he said furiously. "I had no idea you were concerned about my career."

"Why should I be, when you aren't?"

"If I do write another book, you'll probably imagine yourself on every page and sue my socks off."

"I didn't imagine the things you wrote about me in *The Farewell Rock!*"

"They happened to me too. If a writer can't use his own experiences, what kind of book can he write?"

"Well, why don't you go climb a mountain or dive to a sunken ship so you have something exciting to write about?"

He was crossing Main Street bridge at a fast clip, his knuckles white with fury as he clasped the steering wheel.

"You should get a speeding ticket," she said.

"This must be my lucky night!"

She didn't wait for him to open the car door when he stopped across from her apartment, instead dashing out and starting to run across the street. Dropping temperatures had turned the wet snow and slush to ice, and in her haste she didn't see the glassy slipperiness at the end of the drive. Her feet went out from under her, throwing her along the pavement as her purse sailed away. She hurtled sideways, taking the worst impact on her left leg, hip, and arm, but her head hit the street, momentarily stunning her.

"Hessie!"

Adam ran across the street, narrowly escaping the same fate, his leather-soled loafers throwing him into a skid, but he caught his balance and knelt beside her.

"Are you all right?"

"I lost my purse," she said, trying to sit up and wincing from the sharp pain.

"I'll find it. Did you hit your head? Are you dizzy?"

"I'll be okay."

He might forget he was angry in a crisis, but she didn't. Sitting up, she was aware of several sharp pains, but the embarrassment bothered her more.

"Here it is, still zipped shut." He handed her the purse. "Let me help you."

He lifted her off the ice and carried her gently to the door, reassuring her as he carefully navigated the walk and porch.

"We'll see how badly you're hurt, and I'll take you to the emergency room."

"No, I'll be all right."

He let her stand while he unlocked the door, keeping his arm around her when she hobbled to the couch. Her hose were a mass of runs and tears, and the side of her coat was wet and dirty. Slipping out of it, she pinpointed her worst pains: elbow, hip, and thigh. Her back felt achy, and her left shoulder was tender. A little cautious moving made her fairly sure that nothing was broken.

"Is your arm all right?"

Adam's examination was gentle but thorough. Her coat had protected the skin on her arm, but the side of her thigh was badly scraped, blood oozing from the pavement burn.

"Where do you keep your first-aid stuff?" he asked with a concerned frown.

"In the bathroom, but I can manage by myself."

She perched on the edge of the couch, sitting on her already soiled coat and gingerly unzipping the high leather boots that had protected her lower legs, even if they hadn't given her safe footing on the ice.

Adam came back with a stack of towels and her first-aid box.

"Just let me spread a towel so you won't get blood on the couch." He did. "Here, lie on your side."

"I can do this, Adam." She moved too quickly and winced; her threshold of pain was nothing to brag about.

"I'll get some ice packs after I take care of the abrasions," he said, helping to settle her on her side.

"You sound so clinical."

"Red Cross first aid. Everyone should take a course."

"Research for a book?"

"A youthful inclination to fall a lot. Help me slide down your panty hose, what's left of them."

"I can do it. Oh!" Her elbow hurt worse than anything. "Do you think I chipped my elbow bone?"

"Probably not. I'll take you in for an X ray if it's too painful."

"I can wait until morning and take myself."

Peeling off the ripped nylon smarted, but her lack of decorum was bothering her more than the pain. Why couldn't she injure herself in some easy-to-reach part like her knee? Her dignity hit a new low when he took the scissors from the first-aid box and slit her panties up the side, exposing the badly bruised hip and thigh.

She had to give him credit for being gentle and competent,

but the warm towel he used to wash away the grit from the street made her scraped skin burn furiously.

"Brace yourself. I'm going to use this spray," he warned.

"That's nasty stuff," she protested, trying to distract herself by remembering why she'd bought it. Yes, it was supposed to take the sting out of sunburn, but it caused pain on open cuts. The spray hit with torrents of agony, and she bit her lip to keep from shrieking.

After her skin was saturated with germ-killer, he gently probed her hipbone, satisfied when she didn't groan as much as she had for the spray.

"You're going to have some aches and pains."

He brought her two mild pain-killers from the bathroom cabinet, then fixed twin ice packs, doubling food-storage bags to hold the cubes, since she'd never purchased an ice bag. The cold was uncomfortable on her bruises but numbed them after a while. He watched a talk show on her small black-and-white TV, insisting that ice was essential right after an injury. Miserable as she was, she dozed for over an hour.

"I'll help you to bed," he said when she awoke, conscious of dozens of little aches and a couple of big ones.

"No, I'll be all right."

"Your bed is turned down, and I laid out a nightgown. I'm staying until you're settled in. And don't worry about your classes. I phoned Solaski while you were sleeping. I'll teach them tomorrow."

"Absolutely not!" She moved too quickly and tears came to her eyes.

"Easy."

His hand on her shoulder was comforting, but she didn't want it to be.

"You can hardly walk, and you're going to be black-and-blue in places you can't even see. I'm not sure I should leave you alone tonight."

"I insist that you do!"

"I could sleep on the couch."

"No, Adam. Thank you, but no."

Moving slowly and painfully, she got ready for bed, uncomfortably aware of the low hum of the TV in the living room. She came to the door in her robe and told him to go home, but he insisted on tucking her in.

"I'll stop by on my way to the campus, just to make sure you're all right."

"Adam, I've set the clock. I'll teach my own classes."

Her last waking thought was that Adam could be terribly comforting.

CHAPTER EIGHT

Her alarm button was off, but she was sure it hadn't rung. Smarting and aching, she was in too much pain to have forgotten waking up earlier and shutting it off herself.

Gingerly, Hester slid her feet to the floor, digging her toes into the fuzzy blue pile of the throw rug by her bed. It hurt to move, but there was none of the bone-grating pain she remembered from breaking her arm when she was eleven. A big purple bruise above her elbow ached the most, but she was sure X rays were unnecessary.

Clearing the sleepiness from her eyes, she looked at the face of her clock. Her first class started in twenty-five minutes, and she suspected Adam of a new treachery: he'd turned off the alarm before leaving last night so she wouldn't wake up. Why was he so eager to teach her classes?

She was wiggling into her robe when the front door opened and closed, giving her quite a fright. The landlord never used his passkey without warning her ahead of time.

"Hester?"

Her relief at hearing Adam's voice was immediately replaced by anger. She hurried to meet him as fast as her stiff leg allowed.

"Good, you're up," he said.

"You took my key."

"I wanted to be able to get in if you needed me. How're you feeling?"

"Fine," she lied. "Did you turn my alarm off?"

"I thought you could use extra sleep. Solaski was completely agreeable about having me take your classes today."

"I'm not agreeable! I'd much rather do my own work, Adam."

"Let's see your elbow." He rolled up the loose sleeve of her robe and examined the purple bruise. "Can you bend it?"

"You're not a doctor."

"No, but I know enough to take you to one if necessary."

"Oh, wow!" She sat on the nearest chair shaking her head.

"Dizzy?" he asked with concern.

"No, floored. My mother didn't hover over me this much when I fell out of a tree and broke my arm."

"You never told me about that. See how much we still have to learn about each other? I had poison ivy that spread everywhere when I was eight. And at summer camp I tipped over a canoe and hit my head."

"Look, Adam, just go baby-sit with my first class until I get there. I'm fast. I should make the last half easily."

She stood and tried to disguise the fact that walking hurt like the devil.

"And leave my key!"

She'd been too optimistic about getting to her first class. Every move she made hurt, and not even skipping breakfast saved enough time to get there before it was over. She did go to work, finishing the rest of her full schedule with more discomfort than she'd admit to anyone.

Friday she had a respite from Adam, but not from the stiff ache in her hip and leg. When evening came, all she wanted to do was stretch out on the couch with an absorbing novel. Adam had other plans for her. He showed up at her door with two grocery bags, just after she'd changed into a comfortable violet velour lounging robe, intending to eat a sandwich for supper and settle herself for the evening in the least punishing position.

"Steak and fresh mushrooms," he said, carrying his load right to the kitchen.

"I thought we were mad at each other."

"I never stay mad long," he said, grinning.

"I always do."

"But you need me tonight. How do you feel?"

"Fine. I don't need you."

"You always say that." He smiled in disbelief. "I'm sorry our fight made you fall."

"It didn't. I just wasn't expecting that patch of ice."

"More winter ahead. The ten-day forecast is bleak."

"No worse than usual for March, I'm sure."

"Let's see." He was spreading packages all over her counter. "You like your steak medium-well, cooked through but not burnt on the outside."

"Your fantastic memory," she said dryly.

She wanted to lie down, but there was something restful about watching him take charge in the kitchen. In his own way he was quite an organizer. Much of his nonconformity was just his way of getting useless baggage out of his life, she thought, remembering what he'd said about eliminating it from their relationship.

Refusing to accept no for an answer, he settled her on the couch, fluffed pillows, and covered her legs with an afghan, promising to serve dinner there.

"I have some snack trays in the front closet," she said.

"I'll find everything."

She couldn't fault the dinner: broiled steak with barely a tinge of pink, mushrooms sautéed in butter, endive and romaine salad with tarragon vinegar and oil dressing, crusty Vienna bread, and crème de menthe on vanilla ice cream. Adam even insisted on doing the dishes, leaving her to daydream in drowsy contentment on the couch. She'd never been coddled quite this way before; her family was more the stiff-upper-lip type.

Later he sat on the floor beside the couch, his back leaning against the edge, his head so close she couldn't resist fingering the sandy hair that just touched the neck of his navy cashmere sweater. He played an old favorite, *Kismet*, on her

143

tape machine, not breaking the mood of the music with conversation. Arabian love scenes floated through her mind while Adam held her hand against his cheek, occasionally bringing it to his lips for soft little kisses.

When the music ended and he knelt beside her for a long, leisurely kiss, she'd never felt so warmly sensual or totally relaxed. His breath was minty and fresh, and the faint flow of air from his nostrils was a delicious tickle.

When he slowly unzipped the velvety violet robe and reached inside, she guided his hand to the fullness of her breasts under a sheer nylon nightie, sighing with contentment as his hand traveled from peak to valley to peak. He made her feel marvelously cherished, raining soft kisses on her throat while he held the weight of one breast in his hand, stroking with his thumb until fiery darts of longing coursed through her body.

"You're so beautiful," he murmured, still kneeling, favoring her other breast, creating little daggers of warmth that made her tingle all over.

Her bruised side was against the back of the couch, forgotten until she reached out to him and bumped her elbow against the upholstered cushion, bringing an involuntary "oh."

"If I don't stop, I'll hurt you," he whispered regretfully.

"No, I'm fine." She teased the hair behind his ears and slipped lower on the pillows.

"You always say you're fine, but I don't want you to be a martyr for me."

"For myself, then."

He squeezed her breast, reluctant to abandon the pliant mound of flesh.

"It's so nice, just being friends," he mumbled, burying his face in hair that seemed coppery in the dim light and running his fingers up and down a downy-soft slope.

He needed both hands for his next kiss, holding her close while he explored her mouth, finding a sweet response there that made them both giddy with longing.

"Don't ever run away from me again," he said seriously,

drawing back to study her finely chiseled features, touching her cheek with his knuckles.

"It wasn't the smartest thing I've ever done," she admitted, wiggling closer to him, failing to conceal a wince when she hit her thigh on the back of the couch.

"I'm going now," he said softly, "for your own protection. But I'll be taking you with me in my mind, making love to you with every waking thought, and dreaming about you if I'm lucky enough to get to sleep."

"I don't want you to leave."

"I don't want to, but I don't trust myself to make love to you without touching anything on your left side. You'll thank me in the morning."

"Will I see you in the morning?"

"Oh, darn it, no! I have an autograph party in Chicago. I have to leave before dawn, and Sunday I'm scheduled on one of those afternoon panel shows that no one watches. Sometimes I wish I could write a book and forget about it!" He kissed her impatiently, drawing her lips between his for a shivery buss.

She held him in the circle of her arms, feeling aggressive as she never before had with Adam, not wanting him to leave.

"Cancel all that," she urged.

"Tempting." He moved to her foot, bare under the afghan of crocheted granny squares, and caressed the top, trailing little nibbling kisses up her shin to her knee. "You don't know how tempting," he whispered hoarsely.

"I'm practically healed."

"You will be when I get back." He stood, looking more regretful than she'd ever seen him. "I'll see you Monday."

"You'd better. My class is expecting lecture number three. You wouldn't want to disappoint your fans."

"I'd love to disappoint them, if you'll spend the day in bed with me."

"It's still my job, Adam."

"At least promise you'll miss me."

"Starting the instant you leave," she said fervently, bringing his hand to her lips and covering the hard palm with frantic little kisses.

"We can work this out?" he asked hopefully.

"Just kiss me again."

Saying good night was thrilling and frustrating and depressing all at the same time. Monday seemed like a far-distant date.

This time his spell didn't wane. She floated through her weekend, ignoring her aches and pains but hating the purple bruises and raw scraped skin that made her less than perfect for Adam. She spent an hour in the drugstore reading labels on ointments to see if any would help her heal faster. Fortunately, nature did the job for her, so by Monday morning she was walking almost normally.

Her morning freshman class was the first disaster of the day. In his one short hour of substituting, Adam had changed the assignment for the week and given the class an extra two weeks to finish a paper she'd intended to grade before turning in midterm progress reports. For several students it was their last chance to avoid receiving pink warning slips. It took most of the class period to dispel the confusion he'd created. Friday's evening of euphoria was fading fast.

Lecture number three didn't take place as scheduled. Hester was more hurt than angry when Adam wasn't there on time; he'd promised not to be late. She killed time talking about term papers, answering questions, and letting the class members share some of their findings. When it became obvious that Adam wasn't coming at all, she called on her most talkative student, Tammy Philips, for a summary of her research, praising her as a reward and suggesting some pitfalls that novice researchers faced. Leaving the room afterward, Hester felt deeply disappointed. She'd been right all along in not trusting Adam.

Skipping lunch, she tried to tackle some paperwork in her office, but her heart wasn't in it. Outside the window the early thaw had left the campus soiled and dreary-looking. The shrunken snow piles were gray and gritty, with patches of dead grass showing on the lawn. When spring came, the

146

grounds would be lovely, but under the leaden sky of late winter, the view was drab. A student passed below her window in a bright red ski jacket, the only cheerful bit of color in sight, and across the quad by the buff brick science building, a couple were strolling, their heads close together.

Turning back to her papers, Hester suddenly jerked upright and walked to the window to confirm what her subconscious had registered. There weren't many storm coats on Halsted's campus, and even from a distance she could recognize Adam's loose-jointed stride. He was walking with both hands in his pockets, probably gloveless as usual, with his head bent to listen to the petite blonde in a lavender jacket. Adam was walking with Tammy Philips, certainly the star member of his local fan club. While Hester watched in shock, Adam withdrew one hand from a pocket and laid it on Tammy's shoulder. They were so engrossed in conversation that a young man in yellow sweats jogging across campus nearly collided with them.

He couldn't fulfill his obligation to lecture, but he did have time for dazzling coeds. Quickly stepping away from the window, she reeled under the disappointment, standing like a statue as she weighed what it meant. She'd been deluding herself, beginning to trust and lean on Adam when it could only bring her fresh pain.

Dear God, it hurt. Why did love have to have this painful underside, exposing the giver to the worst kind of torment? Surprisingly, she wasn't jealous of Tammy; it was Adam's casual betrayal of her trust that devastated her. Tammy could no more resist his charm than she herself had as a foolish graduate student full of romantic notions. If anything, she felt protective of her student; she didn't want Tammy to suffer because of her crush on Adam.

That evening she had dinner with Constance, then worked at the library until it closed, looking up some references she'd long intended to consult. The phone rang once after she got home, but she didn't answer. Tuesday, too, she avoided her apartment and didn't answer calls. She had her office partner answer their phone, not offering any explanation when she told him to say she wasn't there. In a town the

147

size of Vienne, she couldn't avoid Adam forever, but she needed this respite to remember all the reasons for not trusting him.

Tuesday night Adam was waiting in his car when she came home from a city commission meeting where they'd discussed a joint project with the college. The dean liked his faculty to become involved.

"You've been avoiding me," he said tonelessly.

"Yes, I have."

She opened her door and let him follow her in, knowing she had to face him sometime.

"Do you want to tell me why?"

"I just think Friday was a mistake. Being acquaintances works better."

"Why not admit the truth? I know you're angry about Monday."

"No, I'm not angry. You couldn't get to the lecture. I'm sure you had a perfectly good reason."

"You never wanted me in your class to begin with . . ."

"And I certainly don't want you changing my assignments and deadlines. I have to worry about midterms and pink slips and—"

"I'm sorry for that. The poor kids seemed so overworked. Maybe you're a little too tough on your classes."

"This college has high standards. Its graduates are supposed to be educated!"

"All right! I always was a sucker for a sad story. I was out of line changing your plans. But missing the lecture wasn't my fault."

"Of course not! You probably had a man come to fix your sump pump or paint daisies on your bathroom wall."

"You should avoid sarcasm, Hessie. You're not very good at it."

"And you're not good about doing what you say you will."

"Not when a semi jackknifes and ties up traffic for miles when I'm trying to get out of Chicago!"

"Your show was Sunday afternoon. You could've been back that evening."

148

"I was invited to appear on an early-morning talk show Monday. On a radio station that has a huge listening audience in the Chicago area. You keep me too agitated to write a new book! I have to keep selling the one that's finished."

"So it's all my fault you missed the lecture!"

"Didn't I apologize for that?"

"No, and it really doesn't matter. I prefer to teach my own class."

They were squared off in her living room, both wearing their coats.

"Like it or not, I'll be there Wednesday for number three," he said.

"Number four! The wasted class period counts as your third."

"If that's the way you want it."

"I want to teach my class according to carefully made plans. You didn't give me much choice when you ran to your buddy Solaski."

"If I hadn't, you'd still be stewing about your tenure."

"My friend in the drama department is resigning this spring. I may look for greener pastures myself." She took off her coat; why did the temperature always soar above ninety when she wasn't home?

"You're going to let me drive you away from a job you love?" He sounded scornful and unbelieving.

"Whatever I do, you won't influence my decision one way or another."

"We'll see about that," he said ominously, opening the door to leave.

"Is there any possibility at all that you could be on time Wednesday? If your painters and plumbers can spare you."

He didn't stay to hear more, but she had no intention of saying that she'd seen him with Tammy.

On Wednesday, Adam was waiting in the room when her students arrived. Wearing a three-piece brown suit, a white shirt, and one of the neckties he detested, he puzzled Hester more than he impressed her. What game was he playing now? His lecture was faultless; he used note cards, a bit dog-eared from past use, and kept to the subject, discussing the use of symbolism in twentieth-century novels. When he put effort into it, he was a dynamic speaker. Why did he wait until they were barely speaking to deliver a good lecture?

The class sensed his no-nonsense attitude and busily took notes. Tammy was in the front row writing furiously in a spiral notebook. Hester avoided looking at her.

"This is my last lecture," Adam said when he'd concluded his talk. "I've enjoyed meeting you, and I'd like to become better acquainted."

Hester bit her lip, pretty sure which student he wanted to know better.

"I've been redoing a bungalow on the other side of the river. Since I'm new in town, I'd be honored if you'd join me for a housewarming party Saturday night. Food and beer's on me, and bring a friend if you like. Just so I know how many are coming, I'll pass around this sheet. You might jot down your campus phone number and indicate whether you're bringing a guest."

Sparked by Tammy's enthusiastic response, the young men and women in the class seemed delighted. It didn't take long for the paper to fill with names.

"Ms. Paine, you're invited, of course. I wouldn't dream of having the party without you," Adam said.

"I do have other plans," she answered stiffly.

"Well, I could put the party off for a week."

"No, don't do that," she said quickly, keenly attuned to her students' response. A party two weeks away didn't have the same spontaneous excitement. "I'll manage to be there."

Tammy was staring at her new idol with an infatuated gaze. On second thought, Hester wanted to be at his party. She was fond of Tammy and sincerely wanted her to develop her talents. Maybe there wasn't a thing she could do to protect her promising student from Adam's charisma, but she had a strong feeling that she should try.

She left the room with the students to avoid another confrontation with Adam. He was gregarious, enjoying people of all ages, but Hester was sure there was more behind this party idea than a simple desire to socialize. And why had he canceled the last two lectures? She thought of Solaski's article for the alumni quarterly and decided Adam could explain to her department head if he wanted to; she wasn't going to mention it.

Trying to guess the motives behind everything Adam did gave her a headache that wasn't helped by the damp, chilly atmosphere. She preferred winter to the in-between seasons. Today was dreary, and not even the longer daylight hours compensated for the gray pall that hung over the town. Another good snowfall would be welcome to cover up the muck and debris left behind by the thaw.

CHAPTER NINE

Sooner or later every faculty member had to take a turn promoting Halsted College. Hester was tapped for duty Saturday, asked to appear at a career day for high school seniors; the admissions director who'd planned to go was down with the flu. Dean Williamson had suggested her as a replacement.

Grover was only sixty miles west of Vienne, but the school had scheduled a day-long program. She drove there in her car, loaded with catalogs, pamphlets, and posters picturing campus life. Recruiting was essential to Halsted's survival, as well as to its athletic successes. As higher-education costs soared, students turned to less-expensive state institutions. The small college had to hustle to keep its enrollment up, unable to rely on reputation alone to attract new students.

Hester firmly believed in the merits of the small liberal arts college and was willing to do her part, but the assignment was hard work. She manned a booth from eleven in the morning until four in the afternoon, then participated in an hour of informal socializing before dinner in the school cafeteria. All participating recruiters, including the army and the navy, were expected to speak for two minutes. It was difficult to glorify Halsted over the remains of fried chicken, mashed potatoes, and canned peas. She felt drained when the program was finished.

Spending the day in the gym and the basement cafeteria, she'd hardly noticed the weather, but there was plenty of evidence that it wasn't improving. An inch or so of heavy wet snow shrouded the surface of her car, and under that a thick layer of ice had formed from earlier freezing drizzle. She started the motor and ran the defroster, then tried to chip away the tough shell of ice on the windows. The scraper passed ineffectively over the frozen coating, forcing her to dig ridges with the edge of the plastic tool before she could begin to clear the windows.

When she got back to Vienne, she still had Adam's party to face. The prospect was anything but pleasing; she'd feel like a chaperone. The defroster loosened the ice on the windshield so her scraping went faster, but it still took forever to clear the car. By the time she started driving, wet pellets were bombarding the countryside. The windshield wipers had to labor continuously, and a strong wind was battering the small car.

The character of the storm changed as she drove, the sleety precipitation turning to ordinary snow and accumulating at an alarming rate. The way it was coming down, she'd be lucky to get home before the highway drifted shut in spots. Worse, the pavement underneath the snow was slick, forcing her to drive at a very slow speed. The snow was so thick, she didn't know whether there was more danger ahead or behind. If she drove faster, she might run into a slower vehicle unseen in the blinding storm. Going too slowly put her in jeopardy from a faster car behind her.

Grasping the wheel so tightly that her hands ached, she peered through the swirling whiteness, trying to locate the turnoff into Vienne. Never had a highway sign been so welcome! Approaching the town was even more hazardous; the road curved and the snow had obscured the middle line and the shoulder. She could drive into a farmer's field without realizing it. Two red lights glowed faintly through the thick snow, and she gambled that the driver ahead knew the road better than she did. Keeping the taillights in sight wasn't easy, but following them seemed safer than straying into an oncoming car on the opposite side of the road. At last she

153

recognized a familiar building close to the road, a small factory on the outskirts of town.

The route through the business district and across the river to her apartment still seemed like a long distance, but the worst was behind her. The red lights disappeared after the driver ahead made a right turn, but she screwed up her courage to drive on without a guide. Fortunately there were few cars on the road. Her biggest worry now was that the drifting snow had already blocked some streets. Not even the plows were out!

The last thing on her mind was partying, but she came to a familiar traffic signal and realized she was only blocks from Adam's home. The housewarming had started a couple of hours earlier, but she was exhausted after fighting her way through the dark on blizzard-swept roads. Although a hot bath and a long sleep at home were much more appealing, she knew the smart thing would be to stop for a rest at his gathering. Maybe the storm would stop, and she'd be able to follow a guest, hopefully someone with a four-wheel drive, across the river. Her chances of getting home were decreasing with each block; Main Street had only one lane passable, and she shuddered to think of the side streets with ice under the drifts.

Even when her decision was made, she had a hard time reaching Adam's house. Her car went into a spin when she tried to stop at an intersection, and for a few anxious moments she was afraid the car was stuck. Without her driving experience in Maine, she never would have made it to his driveway.

The bungalow was brightly lit, but visibility was so poor she couldn't see where the guests' cars were parked. Adam undoubtedly kept his New Yorker in the garage at the rear, but the students probably crowded into a few vehicles. The porch light managed to glow through the bombardment of snowflakes, and she was grateful for a chance to rest before tackling the drive across town.

Taking a quick inventory, she decided her outfit was okay for a party with students. She was wearing a muted gold suit with a blouse a darker shade. Adam was right about wearing yellow; she loved every shade from pale lemon to deep gold, and her creamy complexion allowed her to wear them. Her hair was a shambles, though, half up and half down after braving the winds to scrape her windows. She took off one glove and let down the rest of it, arranging it haphazardly on her shoulders. It was the best she could do without a mirror.

Bare sidewalk showed in one patch, but snow had drifted against the steps, making them hard to find. She groped her way up to the porch with extreme caution; even though her bruises had faded to light purple and green, she remembered well the consequences of falling on ice.

Stamping her boots in the confines of the enclosed porch, she noticed the silence. Not many people had gotten to the party, or she'd be able to hear them through the curtained windows. Finding the button for the door chimes, she pressed it with her thumb.

Adam was wearing a burgundy robe and white crew socks, hardly a party outfit, and the room behind him was silent and empty.

"Hessie! I've called your place a hundred times. What are you doing out in this weather?"

"Going to a housewarming, I thought."

"Come in. The party was canceled. I started calling the students late this afternoon when the severe storm warning was broadcast. Where've you been? Damn, you really had me worried!"

"I went to Grover High School for a career day. Recruiting for good old Halsted."

"Where's Grover?"

"About sixty miles west."

"You drove sixty miles in this?" He gestured wildly toward the window.

"There wasn't much choice after I was on the road. I thought your party would be in full swing by now, and you live closer to the highway than I do."

"I can't see across the street. You could've been killed driving in this!"

"Well, the roads were bad, but I had them pretty much to myself. If the party's off, I'll go home."

The prospect of getting back into the car made her feel limp with fatigue.

"Two can have a party."

She was too tired for that suggestion.

"No, I really should go now, Adam."

"There's a travelers' advisory out. The radio is warning people to stay off the streets. It'd be much safer to stay here," he said grimly.

"But I'd like to go home to bed. It's been a hard day."

"Then let me get dressed. I'll drive you."

"Round trip across town? Really, I'll be fine."

"Stubborn Yankee," he said vehemently. "When are you going to learn that there's nothing wrong with needing someone?"

"Thank you for the invitation," she said coolly, noticing for the first time that her boots were dripping on a beautiful earth-tone carpet, the pile thick underfoot. "I'm messing up your new rug."

She left over his protests, wanting to collapse and sleep around the clock. The short delay had been enough to cover her car with snow again, and she took out the brush reluctantly, stepping through deep drifts to clean the windows on the far side. The tire tracks where she'd driven only minutes earlier had almost been swept clean, and the wind whined through old trees lining the street. Her hair whipped wildly around her face, and the howling of the storm seemed unearthly in the absence of human sounds. She could still go back into Adam's house, but her pride wouldn't let her.

Starting the car, she backed slowly toward the street, and that was her big mistake. She needed more momentum to get through the accumulation of snow, and the icy surface underneath foiled her. The car jerked to one side, burying the rear wheels in a drift. She rocked, gunned, and fought to free her lightweight compact, but the tires spun helplessly, digging a deeper pit to hold her there.

Still doggedly determined, she got out to size up the situation. The compact was straddling the sidewalk, backed up against an old wedge of snow that hadn't melted completely. The frozen ridge had served as a wall to catch fresh drifts, and it was going to take more than a little shoveling and a handful of sand to free her vehicle. This wasn't the light, powdery snow she'd sped through in the motel lot at Madison; it was wet, heavy, and nasty. Completely at a loss about what to do next, she watched dejectedly as Adam made his way toward her.

"I was going to offer to help, Hessie, but I don't know. You've really buried those rear wheels. I think you need a tow truck."

"It's not my fault there's solid ice under the snow. You could have salted."

"I wasn't expecting visitors in this blizzard." He had to shout to be heard. "Better come inside."

She didn't have much choice.

"May I use your phone?" she asked after removing her boots and letting them drip on a mat by the door.

"Sure, but you won't get anyone to come tonight."

"I have auto club insurance for emergencies. This certainly qualifies as one."

She made her calls from the kitchen, growing more and more agitated under Adam's watchful stare. Garages simply weren't answering. One had a recorded message to call in the morning.

"No luck?" He knew she hadn't had any.

"I haven't finished calling."

"Suit yourself."

He strolled out of the room, returning a few minutes later without the pants he'd put on before going outside. His robe was velour, and she wondered if he knew how much she loved velvety fabric. That was one thing he hadn't mentioned in his darn book.

"Don't feel bad," he said when she finally gave up. "I'm still in the mood for a housewarming."

"Great," she said wearily.

"I'll make you a drink."

"No! No, thank you." None of that! She'd never forget the night of the dean's party.

"Have you had dinner?"

"The usual chicken and peas." She forced a little half grin.

157

"Some hot chocolate, then."

She went into the bathroom while he made the hot drink, horrified by her reflection in the mirror but delighted with his decorating. He'd done the walls in Wedgwood blue with sculptured white tiles on the bottom half. A huge mirror in a white wicker frame hung over the sink, and the other fixtures were the same wicker: towel racks, clothes hamper, and shelves. There was still a faint, clean scent of fresh paint, and the floor was carpeted in silvery plush. She attacked her hair vigorously with the small brush in her purse, making it flare out with electricity and settle in a fiery mass on her shoulders.

What was she going to do now? Staying all night with Adam was sheer madness, but her car was blocking his. Walking home was out of the question; she'd never make it. Her pulse was racing when she returned to the living room through his office, repainted and carpeted in restful shades of beige and tan but no less cluttered.

The main room of the house had undergone a marvelous transformation. The fireplace stones glistened after a vigorous cleaning, and the blaze on the hearth illuminated the warm creams and browns in the room. Adam hadn't needed her help in picking a lovely crushed velvet living room set a few shades darker than the ivory walls or the graceful occasional tables polished to a honey hue. A brown-striped easy chair and a recliner upholstered in tweedy tan blended into the homey setting. It was a room for relaxing, and she curled up on a corner of the couch, carefully accepting the cup Adam handed her.

"You've done a wonderful job with the house," she said.

"Thanks, but the outside is still dingy pink."

"Winter can't last forever. Have you decided on a color?"

"What do you think?"

"Something neutral maybe? Tan, beige?"

"Safe and conservative," he said agreeably.

"You seem to like those colors inside."

"I think the outside of my bungalow should make a statement."

"Really? What kind of statement?"

"Oh, it should say that interesting people live here. Violet might be nice, about the shade of that robe you were wearing when I cooked dinner."

"Now I know you're putting me on."

"There are some things I don't kid about." He was straddling a low stool, thoughtfully sipping hot chocolate.

They were quiet for several minutes, but there was strain in the silence. The fire and the hot drink should've made her sleepy, but she felt wide-eyed and hyper, in the mood for some vigorous activity. Aware of his eyes following her, she carried her empty cup and his to the kitchen and stood staring out at the backyard.

"Still snowing," he confirmed, flicking a switch near the side entrance that illuminated the first twenty feet of his back property.

"You have a nice big yard."

"Lots to mow," he agreed, "but it gives me privacy. The bushes make a natural fence all around the property when the leaves come. A person could sunbathe without a stitch and not be seen by the neighbors."

"Why would you want a sunburned bottom?" she asked. Summer seemed remote as she watched the snow blowing against the window.

"Some things you accomplish gradually. Wouldn't you like to be honey tan from head to toe?" He was standing very close, his voice a low caress.

She didn't answer. Adam had been in her thoughts for years, but theirs had always been a winter relationship. How would he look in a bathing suit, running through the swell along the beach? Or sunning his length on an inflated mat in his own backyard, soaking up sun through muscles glistening with suntan oil? Her imagination took her a step further, daydreaming about rubbing lotion on his smooth hard shoulders and the swells of his back, trailing down to the little hollow at the end of his spine, covering his cute round buttocks, and sliding over strong thighs and well-formed calves.

This was an alarming image on a stormy March night! If

159

men ever started reading women's minds, the battle of the sexes would never be the same!

Wrapping his arms around her waist, he settled her hips against him, making her wonder why any woman would want a man who towered over her. They were such a good fit, if all that mattered was the way his thighs and torso cushioned her.

"How are your bruises?" he asked softly.

"Not pretty, but not painful either."

"I love this color on you." He ran one hand up the length of her sleeve. "My daring redhead."

She wasn't quite sure how he did it, but her jacket was off. Caressing her arms with a low crooning sound, he nuzzled the back of her neck, holding her so close that she was aware of every muscle in his body.

"Adam . . ."

What had she intended to say? He pushed aside her hair and kissed the side of her neck, massaging her shoulders and upper arms, sliding his knee between hers.

"I redecorated all the rooms," he said softly. "Would you like the full tour?"

"I've seen all but your . . ." Why couldn't she say "bedroom"?

"I went a little wild in that room," he said, leading her by the hand through the living room to the door of the one unseen room.

The bedspread was burgundy, a much deeper and richer shade than his robe, with the sheen and nap of real cut velvet. Mythical figures were embroidered in black silk thread across the expanse of the spread, strange figures in graceful poses. The walls of the room were stark white with oriental prints, black woodblocks on rice paper framed in narrow black frames. The furniture was the same, but it glowed from hard polishing. The carpeting was a light shade of gray, and the surfaces of the desk and dresser were empty except for a set of silver combs and brushes and one Chinese vase.

"This is a side of you I haven't seen," she admitted nervously.

"There are others you don't even suspect," he said, mockingly mysterious.

"Adam, if I could just borrow your couch tonight."

"Anything you like."

He hadn't replaced the old-fashioned frosted ceiling fixture, and the light was dim. Staring for a moment at his room, she didn't notice that he'd moved to the doorway, leaning against the jamb and filling the entrance with his broad shoulders.

"If you have a sheet and blanket . . ." She faltered, unable to meet his gaze.

"Plenty," he said. "Come here."

"Oh, no! I know what happened last time you gave me an order like that."

"Something terrible happened?"

"No." She sighed deeply, wishing she'd taken some acting courses.

He stretched out his hand. Intending to brush past him, she found her fingers intertwined with his, her palm pressed against his harder one.

"Do you approve?" he asked.

"Of your decorating? It's marvelous."

"Then it wasn't such a folly to buy this house?"

"It's very nice now," she admitted reluctantly.

"I'll get some bedding for the couch."

Returning in a few minutes, he carried a stack of sheets, blankets, and a pillow.

"You're probably exhausted after that drive," he said sympathetically.

"Yes." She had been; now she was more jittery than sleepy.

"I don't wear pajamas, so I can't loan you my tops. Would you like a terry-cloth robe?"

"I'd appreciate it." Why was she so uneasy when Adam was being the perfect host?

"Shower if you like. I think I'll read until you're ready for bed."

She took advantage of his offer, standing under the warm spray until she felt calm and drowsy. Her hair was wet anyway, so she shampooed it, toweling it dry after she rubbed her body to a pink glow on a thick white towel. Barefoot and wearing his yellow terry robe, she tiptoed back to the living room, surprised that he seemed to be dozing on the recliner.

Spreading out the sheets and blankets on the couch, she glanced, perplexed, in his direction. Should she wake him before lying down? The fire was reduced to orange coals, giving off just enough glow for her to see the outlines of the furniture when she turned off the ceiling lights. Adam didn't snore, she noticed, wondering again if she should wake him or cover him. She decided on the latter, taking one of the three blankets he'd brought for her use and carefully draping it over his length.

"Thank you." His lids were half open, and he moistened his lips with the tip of his tongue.

"You're awake. You can go to bed."

"I have your permission?" he teased.

"I only meant . . ." There wasn't any good way to explain that she'd feel much safer when he was behind a closed door.

"You'd like to get rid of me?"

"I wouldn't have put it quite that way."

"I won't leave without a good-night kiss." He put his hands behind his head, watching with an expression she couldn't decipher in the nearly dark room.

"Then you take the couch, and I'll sleep in your bed," she teased.

"I never intended to make you use the couch."

"I was kidding!"

"I'm not."

"It's a very nice couch."

"You're a very nice woman. Would one kiss be so terrible?"

It wouldn't; that was the trouble.

"Blackmail?"

"No, desperation." He didn't move a muscle.

"One kiss?"

"One."

She leaned over him feeling like a parachuter making a first jump.

"Ummm." He moaned with satisfaction when she lightly touched his lips with hers.

"It wasn't that good! You're exaggerating." She backed away.

"I was sighing over the promise."

"There wasn't any promise. That was a platonic kiss."

He pulled the lever that retracted the footrest on the recliner and stood, lazily stretching with his arms high above his head.

"Platonic doesn't work with us, darling. Go crawl into my bed; I'll sleep out here."

"No, the couch is fine for me."

"This is one argument I intend to win."

He advanced menacingly, lowering his shoulders and sweeping her up with one catlike movement. Before she could struggle, she was flung over his shoulder, her head and arms dangling helplessly behind his back.

The trip to his bed was short but jarring, and he deposited her on top of the spread with a bounce that made the bed shake. Before she could squirm free, he'd straddled her hips, pinning her arms above her head. The borrowed robe and her slip under it were bunched at the small of her back, and she felt the deliciously slippery velvet on her legs. She rubbed her heel over the luxurious nap, confused by the pleasurable sensations bombarding her.

"Now don't be mad," he said, "and I'll let you go."

"Oh, I am mad, very mad, furious, outraged." The words tripped lightly off her tongue without a speck of truth. She was anything but angry, wishing only that she could see Adam's face instead of the dark outline of his head.

"Then I don't dare let you go, do I?" he teased.

"It could be very dangerous," she purred.

"Should I take a calculated risk?" he asked, releasing her arms.

"That depends on how brave you are."

"I'm cowardly when it comes to you."

"That's hard to believe," she whispered.

"I'm constantly afraid of losing you again."

He kissed her softly and sweetly, pressing her head deeper into the velvet-covered pillow. Straightening on his knees, he reached to the side and turned on a bedside lamp.

Visions of turbaned sultans and sultry concubines flashed through her mind; she could almost hear the song of a nightingale and the soft notes of a lyre. Imagining the scent of jasmine and orange blossoms made her dizzy with longing. She knew that she'd come through the blizzard for this.

Adam stood naked beside the bed, thrilling her with his masculine beauty, watching for the invitation she couldn't deny him. She sat and stripped off the robe, wondering why she'd thought a lacy slip and panties were armor against her own desires. When the flimsy garments lay in a pile on the floor, she stretched against the shimmering velvet, then rolled to her tummy and stretched again, delighting in the sensuous caress of the nap and in his throaty chuckle of enjoyment at her antics. Hester could see his flicker of disappointment when she stood on the opposite side of the bed, but he smiled and helped when she started to fold the spread.

"It's beautiful," she said.

"You're beautiful."

Love could be very simple, she thought.

"I've never seen black satin sheets," she said, shivering for a moment from the slippery coolness.

"I've never owned any before. I had a little free time in Chicago."

He gathered her in his arms, showering tiny kisses on her shoulders and neck. She nuzzled his throat above the hard ridge of his collarbone, flicking her tongue with feline quickness over this vulnerable spot.

So relaxed she was limp, she surrendered to him, adding spice with her mischievous sense of humor and her eagerness to be all she could for him. She loved his legs, rough and hairy against her long smooth limbs, and basked in his attentions, woozy with happiness as he caressed her.

"We're not wasting time now, are we?" she whispered, growing more aggressive under his gentle tutelage.

"No time with you is wasted."

With the howling wind as background music, they became frantic with desire, each touch stoking a fire that grew hotter and hotter. She still wanted Adam to run on a wild deserted beach, but now the waves that received his plunging body swept through her, undulating currents of pure joy, rocking her universe.

Damp, spent with passion that left them euphoric, locked together under the snug white blanket she'd first seen on his bed, they curled together for the night. Adam slept; Hester didn't want sleep to obliterate what had happened. She lay there loving him, breathing in rhythm with the rise and fall of his chest, lightly caressing the warm skin sprinkled with wiry hairs and the rose-tinged brown nipples, touching the tips with her finger without waking him.

Locked in the embrace of the man she loved, she forgot the doubts, distrust, and reservations, wholly content as she had never before been in her life.

Adam was right; morning was the nicest time of all. Waking up beside him was as satisfying as a dozen encores at a fabulous concert. They came together in a sleepy daze that only prolonged and heightened their pleasure. She loved everything about his body: the obvious strength, the salty tang of his skin, the heady blend of cologne and natural musk, and the thick sandy hair falling in an unruly mass on his forehead. His waist was slender and his stomach lean except for a little wrinkle above his navel that she loved to tease.

"Ummm, I love natural redheads," he said, fanning her hair over the black satin of the pillow.

"Not all of them, I hope." She pretended to snap at his nose with her teeth.

"Only this one."

He invited her to shower with him, but didn't grumble when she begged for a few more minutes of slumber while he took one by himself. She snuggled under the covers, basking in a sense of well-being, wondering why she didn't want to share the shower with Adam. After last night, how could she feel shy about doing anything with him?

The trouble was, she mused, that highs never lasted, and

165

there was still her car stuck in a drift, a job made more difficult by Adam's interference, and all kinds of complications. She was sorry when she heard the familiar racket of a city plow going down the narrow residential street. Being snowbound had removed her from everyday concerns and troubles. She envied couples stranded together through long winter months where the real world couldn't intrude.

He came into the room, a towel around his waist and wet hair clinging to his head.

"The plow went through." He sat on the edge of the bed.

"Yes, I heard it."

"It didn't do much for your car, though. There's a ton of snow at the end of the drive. Your car is half buried."

"I'll help dig it out. I'm an old snow-shoveler from way back."

"Darling, I have no intention of moving tons of heavy wet snow so you can leave me."

She sat up, self-consciously pulling the black sheet up to her chin. "You mean you won't help me get my car out?"

"Wouldn't you feel guilty if I strained my back?"

"There's nothing wrong with your back," she said, looking at him suspiciously.

He sat beside her, smiling nonchalantly. "I'll call someone to plow my drive."

"All right, but I could get it out with a little help from you."

"Ummm." He stretched out beside her, leaning on one elbow and twisting a lock of her hair around his finger.

"Shouldn't you call for a plow now?"

"There's no rush, is there?" He ran his hand over her breast, tracing the outline of her nipple under the black satin.

"All the garages will have waiting lists."

"If I call for you," he asked, patting her thigh, puckering the sheet over it, "will you stay right here?"

"Let me take a shower."

"All right," he said grudgingly, "but then we'll have breakfast in bed."

"Eat in bed! That sounds so decadent!"

"You Yankees! You'd like to see me chopping wood and hauling water at the crack of dawn."

"Call a plow, please, Adam." She kissed his brow and made a little wet trail with her tongue down the length of his nose.

Putting on yesterday's clothing spoiled the freshening effect of the shower, but she dressed quickly, coming into the kitchen to find Adam still speaking on the phone, an edge of annoyance in his voice.

"Well, if your husband finishes with his regular customers before dark, will you give me a call?" He listened for a moment, then recited his phone number.

"It's not my fault," he said, turning to her after hanging up the receiver of the wall phone. "Snowplowers are having a field day. We'll be lucky to get someone by tomorrow morning. You're stuck with me today, darling."

"There must be someone available," she said frowning. "Aren't you cold?"

He'd exchanged the towel for his burgundy robe, but his legs and feet were bare.

"I was counting on you to warm me. I like that suit, but it's not what a lady wears for breakfast in bed."

"Be serious, Adam. I have to get my car out and go home."

"I thought we could spend the day together and get some things settled," he said invitingly.

"Things?"

"Like when you'll move in, and whether you like your eggs soft-boiled."

"You're just assuming I'm here to stay?"

Things were happening too fast! She needed time to think.

"You didn't come here last night expecting a party," he gravely accused her.

"Adam, I did. I expected to find my students here—at least some of them. I think Tammy Philips would go through more than a blizzard to spend time with you."

"Tammy Philips?"

"Don't pretend you don't know her! I saw you walking

167

with her on campus. On the day you didn't show up for your lecture!"

"Ah." He sat back on one of the leather-top bar stools clustered around an island counter, his breakfast nook. "Where were you?"

"In my office. I just happened to look out the window."

"And you saw me with your little student and assumed the worst?"

"Oh, don't be silly!" She regretted mentioning it.

"So you came through the worst snowstorm of the winter to chaperone."

He was uncomfortably close to the truth.

"I came because I was invited. I hoped one of your guests might lead me home, maybe in a four-wheel drive."

Ramming his hands into the pockets of his robe, he loosened it to expose his chest, the hairs thick and darker than those on his head.

"Just to get it out of the way, I didn't meet Tammy by design. I came to the campus to apologize for missing your class. She asked me some very interesting questions about a paper she's writing. They were complicated but worth answering."

"Of course."

"Jealousy doesn't flatter you, Hessie, although I admit it strokes my ego. Anyway, she suggested coffee, and I went. I decided a little cooling-off time before I saw you wouldn't be a bad idea. I'm wary of redheads when they lose their tempers. That's all there was to it."

"I believe that."

"You do?"

"Why shouldn't I?"

"Tammy's pretty."

"Of course she is. And smart too."

"Then you don't mind that I had coffee with her?"

"Not at all. I have no claim on your time."

"Hester! You have every claim on me, whether you like it or not!" He tried to take her in his arms, but she evaded him, walking to a counter crowded with small appliances, canisters, and an enameled breadbox, a modern reproduction sim-

168

ilar to her grandmother's old tin one with air holes on the sides.

"Do you have a teakettle?"

"No, a saucepan will have to do, but I'll make breakfast after we settle this."

"Adam, there's nothing to settle. You had coffee with Tammy. I don't mind at all, as long as her crush on you doesn't interfere with her plans to get a master's degree."

"So you really came here last night to protect Tammy!"

"That sounds a little melodramatic!"

"Do you have any idea how stupid that makes me feel? I had some weird idea that you wanted to be with me."

"Adam . . ."

The door chimes took them both by surprise. Adam pulled the lapels of his robe together, tightened the belt, and went to answer it.

From the kitchen Hester could hear his conversation, and a glimpse showed two boys in parkas and ski caps, shovels over their shoulders. They offered to clear the drive and free the car for a price that Hester thought was highway robbery. Adam agreed immediately without haggling, asking only that they begin immediately.

"You're about to be rescued by two knights fresh out of puberty," he said sarcastically. "If you're hungry, there are twelve pizzas in the freezer, a keg of beer in the basement, and enough pop and snacks to last through the winter. I'm getting dressed."

She heated water after locating some tea bags in the cupboard. Adam never drank tea. It didn't help her mood to find this proof that he expected company for breakfast. Hadn't she done exactly what he'd wanted in coming to his house? She made toast and dribbled some honey onto it, eating mechanically and listening to the scraping rhythm of shovels on pavement.

Adam came into the kitchen dressed in jeans and a bulky gray sweater, pouring a bowl of cereal for himself and curtly asking if she wanted any.

"No, thank you. I'll pay the boys for the shoveling." She

169

finished the tea in her cup, refusing to look at him. "It's my car they're digging out."

"It's my driveway. I'll pay them."

"At least let me pay half."

"Damn it, Hester, I don't care if you pay off the national debt, but I'll take care of the shoveling!"

"You didn't learn as much as I thought from your mother!"

She knew his angry outburst had nothing to do with money for the boys, but they'd gone from lovers to combatants so quickly, she was totally confused. All she wanted to do was go home and think about their relationship. She loved Adam! She loved being with him! Why did he push her so hard?

"I only want to go to my apartment to see if everything's all right," she explained lamely.

"Unless the place went up in smoke, I don't see what the urgency is. You don't have classes today to use as an excuse." He dumped the remains of his cereal in the sink and started the garbage disposal.

"You just assume that I have nothing important to do! I promised to feed my neighbor's fish, and they haven't had any food since yesterday morning."

"All this fuss about going home for some fish?" There was no trace of humor or understanding on his face. "I don't suppose that neighbor is the coach?"

"They're his tropical fish, but if he were home, I wouldn't be feeding them!"

Now he was making her feel guilty about the fish! Until a few moments ago, she'd completely forgotten them. How long could fish live without food? She was mildly horrified at the thought of Russ returning to find his expensive beauties floating on top of the tank.

"Just being a good neighbor," Adam said dryly.

She wanted to shake him!

The rasp of the shovels seemed to go on forever. Adam went into his office, leaving her to wait by herself. She tried to read a magazine but ended up watching the two young men as they labored to remove a small mountain of snow

170

blocking the drive. The way they lifted their shovels, the snow had to be as heavy as bricks. At last they came to the door for their pay, summoning Adam from his office with the door chimes.

"Why are you so angry?" she asked as he closed the door after paying them.

"I'm not angry," he said sharply.

"You're not happy."

"Damn it, Hessie, nothing between us goes quite the way I plan it."

"What did you plan for last night?"

"I thought after the kids left, we could talk."

"And go to bed! You thought you could talk me into it after the party!"

"Is that really what you think? That all I want is to sleep with you?"

She didn't, but his tone of voice ignited her temper. "How convenient that I fell into your lap after the party was canceled!"

"Any woman with common sense would've stayed overnight in Rover or Dover or whatever place it was. You must've been pretty darn anxious to chaperone my party to drive through a blizzard to get here!"

"I'm used to winter driving. I've never let a little snow bother me."

"A little! It's only blind good luck that you didn't go into a ditch or get squashed on the front of a semi. I was worried enough without knowing that you were doing a macho-woman number on the highway."

"You don't need to worry about me—ever!"

She thrust her feet into her boots, pulling the zippers so hastily that her hose caught in one and it refused to budge upward or downward. Adam watched with disgust on his face.

"You expect me to believe you can handle anything, and you can't even operate a zipper."

He dropped to his knees beside her, grabbing the boot and furiously tugging at the zipper tab.

"Stop it, Adam." She struggled to free her foot, nearly toppling over in her fury.

The harder he tried, the more nylon got stuck in the teeth. "You're not helping a thing!" she cried, frantic now to get away from him.

"Fix it yourself, then," he said angrily, retreating to his office again and closing the door.

She fled the bungalow with her coat open, her hands bare, and her boot half zipped, starting the car with difficulty because she was too upset to concentrate on it. The dingy pink stucco seemed to mock her, and she drove away with hot tears filling her eyes.

Her apartment was stuffy, but she didn't notice. Like a robot programmed for one task, she went up to Russ's apartment and reread his precise list of instructions, feeding the exotic little water creatures who flashed through the aquarium, their brilliant coloring a treasure of nature. Were fish happy? Did they have big enough brains to know when they were miserable? She sat watching them for a long time, wondering why her own life was so complicated. Adam loved her, and she loved him. If they were fish, they could swim away their lives together, blowing bubbles, flicking tails, and acting out their mating ritual in a predestined pattern. The human species was the only one that didn't act by instinct alone, and men seemed to go by a different set of rules than women.

Maybe Adam had a right to be angry. She had come to his house to check up on him, afraid that he'd unintentionally hurt her favorite student. But was he so blameless that he could be self-righteous? He'd written about her most cherished memories, wormed his way into her life, and interfered in her work without once considering if she wanted him to help with her classes or check on her tenure.

More depressed than ever, she went back to her own apartment, lay down on the bed, and slept through the daylight hours. Not surprisingly, she found it impossible to sleep again at the normal time, and the small hours of the morning found her laboring over her boot, which she'd removed from her foot only by taking off the ruined panty hose with it. Finally, using her manicure kit, she freed the nylon without ruining the zipper. She didn't have the vaguest idea why she was crying over a boot.

CHAPTER TEN

Two days, three days, four days: without Adam they blurred together without form, shape, or purpose. She existed and went through the motions of living, but her heart was like a pewter candy mold, cold metal surrounding a hollow nothingness.

A hundred times that week she picked up the phone, yearning to call him but utterly at a loss for words. They were like rival armies on two sides of a mountain pass, each guarding a cold outcrop of rock and depriving the other of the warmth, comfort, and gaiety to be found in the valley. Separation meant misery, but she didn't know how to get rid of their barricades. Starting fresh hadn't worked, and she felt nothing but gloom about the future.

She did discover a hidden talent: acting ability. The routine of her job demanded a strenuous performance as she pretended that everything was normal. Constance, more perceptive than most, challenged her several times, but Hester managed to persuade her busy friend that everything was perfectly normal.

The letter, like the valentines, was lying between the two doors to her apartment. There was no mistaking the scrawly handwriting on the envelope: Ms. Hester Paine. Was Adam mocking her with formality?

She was early for work; there was no reason not to read

his letter before going to the campus, but she was afraid to open it. There was something alarmingly final about the plain white business envelope, the thickness suggesting that several pages were inside.

Placing it in her purse, she was torn between gnawing apprehension and burning curiosity. She'd read it in her office before classes started.

Brad usually respected the imaginary line separating their desks, but she arrived to find the whole office in chaos, her own desk covered with his piles of printed pages.

"Sorry about your desk, Hester," he said without a trace of embarrassment. "I've been here since six A.M. trying to get these pages collated before my first class. It's a new study on faculty salaries. You wouldn't have a few free minutes, would you?"

He looked so haggard, working in shirt sleeves with the gray shadow of a beard on his usually smooth chin and dark circles under his eyes, that she agreed to help him until her first class. Adam's letter stayed in her purse, not forgotten but still unread. When she opened that envelope, she wanted to be alone.

Lunch with Constance was her best tonic, and she didn't want to forgo it today. The drama teacher couldn't contain her excitement about touring in a play, and Hester often wished she had the same daring attitude about Adam. Sometimes she hated her granite-like Yankee conservatism, which forced her not only to look before she leaped, but to measure the drop-off and weigh the consequences. Looking back, she couldn't remember making any wildly reckless decisions in her whole life. She seemed born to calculate and consider every step.

She didn't have a moment alone all day to read the letter in her purse. Returning late in the afternoon, she was relieved to find that Brad had removed himself and his reports from the office, leaving only an overflowing ashtray as evidence of his harried activity. Between his salary studies and the steady stream of articles whipped into shape on the old Royal typewriter they shared, he had a minimum of time left for his classes.

Sitting on the edge of her desk chair, she located the letter and neatly slit the top of the envelope with a silver-plated letter opener her aunt had given her one Christmas. Steeling herself for the worst, she started to read.

My darling Hessie,

While unpacking books, my last and favorite job, I found a little book, *The Complete Letter Writer*, published in 1851. I bought it on impulse years ago in one of those dingy used-book shops in New York City and, when the front cover fell off almost immediately, was mad at myself for paying five dollars. It's a little smaller than a modern paperback with board covers and a deteriorating leather spine, and inside, almost every page has foxing, those brownish-red marks that make a book look like it has measles.

It was a practical little book when it was published, really just a collection of sample letters on everything from business and law to love and courtship, but the fact that I bought it for no reason whatsoever long before meeting you has made me a believer in fate.

There's a verse in the front of the book:

"Heaven first taught Letters for some wretch's aid,
Some banished lover, or some captive maid:
They live! they breathe! they speak what Love inspires
Warm from the heart, and faithful to its fires!"—Pope.

Everything I've done to convince you of my love seems to have backfired, and it took this worn little volume to show how I'd neglected my one persuasive talent: writing. This is my love letter to you.

Aside from inspiring me, the book hasn't been that much help in writing this. You probably wouldn't be impressed to read that I've been "ruminating on your many accomplishments." I can hear your laughter if I tried to describe "the variety of passions now struggling

176

in my breast." So, with great thanks to its author, James M. Alden, I'm closing the little book of letters, thrown back on my own sentiments.

I love you, Hester Paine. You see, there's still no better way to say it. Our meeting illuminated what was then the darkest period of my life, and losing you dropped me into a black pit of despair. *The Farewell Rock* was more than a memorial to our love; it was my way of saying "Come back to me, Hessie." I won't apologize for taking our romance into the realm of fantasy; I'm not a saint or a celibate, content with a spiritual joining of minds. Your body is exciting and beautiful, and I can't look at you without wanting to make love. But there's more, much more, that I love about you.

This is the part of the letter I dread writing, but any explanation that doesn't include my first marriage is meaningless. Joanna and I grew apart. Her dancing was her life, and I never shared any part of it. It wasn't just the separations, although one European tour lasted nearly four months. Feeling shut out of the most important part of her life, I harbored resentments that only pushed her farther away from me.

It's true that Joanna left me, but all I felt was relief. Our relationship was dead. The hard part was facing up to my share of responsibility for the failure of our marriage. I needed time to regain my confidence; I had to be sure I wouldn't fail a second time. I loved you too much to offer you anything but the best part of my life. I had to go slowly because you meant so much to me.

Now, knowing how much I love you, my hesitation seems ridiculous, but, Hessie, at the time I was saddled with an ugly load of guilt, afraid that I'd mess up a beautiful relationship if I didn't put my life on an even keel before going to you.

It wasn't easy to face my own failure, even after my love for Joanna was dead. One obvious reason for the divorce was that we never shared our lives. I was determined to share everything with the wonderful woman I love: you.

I overdid it. Meeting Solaski, meddling in your classes, trying to mastermind your tenure, all were poor attempts to be part of your life.

Darling, I hate teaching: lectures, exams, grades, the whole business. I gladly leave it in your much more patient and capable care. Without my publisher and agent prodding me to sell books, I'd sit home and grow broad in the stern.

This is a very small town, and you're happy here. The two of us living here apart will never work. I want you to live with me, to love me the way I love you. If that can't be, then Vienne will never be my home.

There wasn't a section in *The Complete Letter Writer* about issuing ultimatums; I got my first lesson from a fiery young graduate student on a windy beach in Maine. Hessie, I desperately want to see you this evening. If you feel there's no hope for us, stay away, and I'll have to accept your decision. Tomorrow I'll leave for the west and a warmer climate.

How to end this letter? Would you believe my little nineteenth-century letter-writing guide does it best?

"I am your sincere lover."

Adam

A love letter! She pressed it to her bosom like a maiden in hoopskirts and spit curls and tried not to cry. A hesitant little knock on the closed office door was about as welcome as a party invitation from the dean.

"Come in," she said hoarsely.

"Ms. Paine." Tammy came in slowly with none of her

usual liveliness, her small face pinched and worried. "I have a real problem, and I don't know what to do."

"About your research paper?" Hester glanced at her watch, upset that it was already after six and Adam was waiting for her.

"Oh, no, nothing to do with class. I called your home and just prayed you might still be here."

"What's wrong?"

Tammy was sometimes emotional, but now she looked stricken.

"My roommate is missing!"

"Are you sure? She didn't leave for the weekend without telling you?"

"No! She didn't sleep in our room last night, and I haven't seen or heard from her all day."

"Did you report it to your residence director?"

"Yes, and I called her parents, everyone she's gone out with lately, even the police. Everyone tells me she'll turn up, but I'm scared, Ms. Paine. Jenny and I are good friends. She wouldn't go without telling me!"

"You're right to be worried," Hester agreed, realizing that Adam's letter was still clutched on her lap. As desperate as she was to see him, she had to help Tammy. "Did you tell her parents she's missing?"

"No, her mother gets pretty hysterical over every little thing. I was afraid of what she'd do if she knew Jenny was missing. I pretended to be an old friend who wanted to get in touch with her."

"That's probably best for now. We'd better see the dean and let him talk to the police."

At ten o'clock Hester was at the police station with a sobbing Tammy. The dean was in conference with the chief of police, setting in motion an official search. Together they'd talked to every girl they could find on Jenny's dorm floor and checked all her favorite places. No one had the slightest idea where she was. The dean made a call to her parents, so staidly reassuring that the mother reacted calmly. For the first time, Hester admired his talents.

There really was nothing she could do, but Tammy clung

179

to her, needing her strength and reassurance. A vivid imagination like hers was no asset in a crisis. She was sure her roommate had been abducted or ravished or both. Driving her car, Hester took Tammy back to the dorm, where they were bombarded with questions from the other girls.

By midnight Tammy was cried out, the other girls had divided the town's recreation spots and were combing them for clues the police might overlook, and Hester was watching Tammy call young men her roommate knew. There seemed to be quite a long list of these.

When Tammy went down the hall for a minute, Hester quickly dialed the phone in her room, hanging up on the eighth ring when Adam didn't answer. Had he given up and left? She wanted terribly to go to his house, but Tammy returned and begged her to stay, fearing that the police were going to bring her some terrible news.

Jenny returned at 2:00 A.M. The police were notified, the dean personally called the worried parents, and Jenny was ordered to appear in his office Monday morning for an official appointment. The girls in the dorm, back from their fruitless search, mobbed the room, exploding with questions after Jenny made a duty call to her parents.

"Where have you been?" Tammy demanded of her roommate.

Hester quietly left, not wanting to hear all the details of a romantic escapade that had taken Jenny to Madison on the spur of the moment and left her stranded there.

Adam's house appeared to be dark from the street. If he was gone, she had no way of reaching him. Could he sleep through a ringing phone? She fervently hoped he had.

The door between the porch and the living room had a large glass panel, curtained on the inside but thin enough to let her hear the chimes that summoned him. She pushed the button a second and a third time, finally trying the handle. The door wasn't locked. Not caring whether she had a right to open it, she entered the house, stunned by what she saw flaming on the hearth.

"Adam!"

"I wondered if it was you."

180

"You could've answered the door. What are you doing?"

He was sitting in front of the fireplace, surrounded by low piles of books, the room dark except for the fire in the grate.

"I'm burning my bridges behind me, in this case my books."

Coming closer, she saw the stacks of books, watching in horror as he took a mint copy of *The Farewell Rock* and threw it on the fire, scattering coals in an explosion of orange sparks.

"You're burning your own books!"

"Every last damned copy! If I could, I'd burn every one in print." He threw another book, which threatened to smother what was left of the blaze.

"You have no idea how difficult it is to burn fifty copies of a book that thick."

Hester found the light switch that turned on the ceiling fixture, not sure what to make of Adam's strange behavior. She dropped her coat on a chair and moved closer to him.

"Why burn your own books?"

"Why are you here?" He ignored her question.

"I got your letter."

"Oh? I'm surprised to hear that."

"Adam, stop acting this way!"

"I'm not acting."

He was still sitting cross-legged in front of the fireplace, wearing tan cotton slacks and a black knit turtleneck. Without looking in her direction, he threw another book on the fire.

"Don't burn your books!"

She rushed forward and picked up several, carrying them to the far side of the room and dropping them on a striped chair.

"I paid over fifteen dollars for a copy with a torn dust jacket!"

Without looking in her direction, he asked belligerently, "Why buy a damaged copy?"

"Because I was so upset when I saw your new book, I accidentally ripped it!"

He tossed another book, creating an explosion of sparks

181

that threatened to fly far enough to scorch the carpet. The screen was open and the dark tiles in front of the hearth had bits of ash scattered over them.

"Adam, don't!" She rescued another stack of books, carrying this one to the kitchen and hiding it in a cupboard with pots and pans.

"Are you here for some reason besides rescuing my ill-fated novels?" he asked sarcastically.

"I came because of your letter!"

"Let's see, assuming you opened your door at eight A.M., you mulled over the contents of my inspired epistle for"—he paused—"eighteen hours and twenty-seven minutes. Not what I'd call an instant reaction."

"You've been drinking," she said, trying to find an excuse for his odd behavior.

"I destroyed the better part of a fifth of Scotch, but that was before midnight. Since then I've had two pots of black coffee. Where were you at midnight, Hester? More fish to feed?"

Another novel crashed into the grate, the dust jacket flaming up and engulfing the cover.

"I can't stand this!"

She tried to grab the remaining stack, but he was too quick, taking them into his arms and tossing another one to fiery extinction.

"Then leave," he said harshly.

"Adam! You are so unfair! Did you get me here to make me more miserable than I was?"

"I don't believe you care enough about me to be even mildly unhappy."

"That's a terrible thing to say! I couldn't come sooner. I was—"

"No, no, don't tell me. I understand all about feeding fish and grading papers and all those crushing responsibilities of yours."

"You are vile and horrid and—"

"Disappointed." He stood and faced her, still clutching the remaining novels against his chest. "At six o'clock I was ready to welcome you with the key to my heart and my house. At eight I was worried, and by ten I was angry enough to turn you over my knee. That was a long time ago. Now I'm stone sober, and I don't give a damn about your excuses. You've put me through hell tonight!"

"I didn't even read your letter until six o'clock!"

"And of course you rushed right over to tell me what a fool I'd made of myself!"

"No, Adam! I loved your letter! Oh, why didn't you answer your phone?"

"It never rang."

"I called you. At midnight or a little later."

"I went outside for a few minutes to clear my head," he admitted. "Before the black coffee."

"I was calling from the dorm to tell you what happened, and—"

"The dorm?" he interrupted, pacing the room, stopping to throw another book on the fire.

"Will you stop that!"

She tried to take the books away from him, succeeding only in making him more determined to destroy them. He brushed her aside and sent the remaining four books to the flames in another explosion of sparks.

"Of all the childish stunts!" she cried.

"It's your fault I'm burning them!"

"You're burning them because I objected to—"

"To having all your personal feelings commercialized! Isn't that the way you put it?"

"Yes, but—"

"But your Yankee stinginess hates to see dollars go up in smoke!"

"No, oh, damn you, Adam! You're spoiling everything!"

She covered her face with her hands and turned away, but nothing could stop the shattering sobs. For the first time since she was a toddler, she let another person see her weep, turning away but not able to hide the convulsive shuddering of her shoulders.

"Hessie." He sounded stunned. "Hessie, I've never seen you cry."

He wasn't going to now! She ran to the bathroom, slam-

183

ming the door and turning the lock, perching on the edge of the clothes hamper, and sobbing uncontrollably. His knocking on the door only made her cry more.

"Hessie, let me in!"

She couldn't answer. He didn't even want to know why she hadn't come sooner.

"Darling." He came through the office door.

"Crazy bathroom," she blubbered. "Who ever heard of a john with two doors?"

"I've never seen you cry like this," he said again, sounding awestruck.

She stood and caught a glimpse in the mirror of her face, red and blotched with swollen eyes. The neatly coiled hair on her head couldn't possibly belong to the tear-racked face and flaming cheeks.

"It never occurred to you that maybe I couldn't come sooner," she said brokenly.

"Cry," he said, pressing her face against his shoulder. "Cry, darling. Maybe I'll join you."

He wasn't making fun of her. When she looked up, his eyes looked wet.

"I'm a mess." She desperately needed a tissue, but all she could see was the roll on the wall.

"My handkerchief." He handed her a clean but unironed square of cotton.

"Thank you."

He ran cold water on a cloth and pressed it against her forehead, looking as miserable as she felt.

"Cried out?" he asked anxiously, leading her to the living room.

"I hope so."

The pages of the books made feathery ashes that floated through the opening and onto the tiles. Adam belatedly closed the mesh screen while she moved toward her coat.

"You're not going!" He took the coat away and impatiently tossed it aside.

"I thought my welcome had been withdrawn."

"Look." He rubbed his stinging eyes, tired from staring into the fire as he destroyed the novels. "This time I'm not going to say we should start over. We need to go on from here."

"Do you want to know why I didn't come sooner?" she asked in a small timid voice that didn't seem to belong to her.

For the first time she admitted that she was a little afraid of Adam. If he took his love away, he could hurt her beyond imagining. She thought he felt the same way. Unless they could build a bridge over this chasm, there wasn't any hope for them.

"Please tell me." He took her hand and led her to the couch, sitting down beside her but not releasing his grasp.

"I read your letter in my office around six o'clock. I wanted to be alone when I did, and that was my first chance." She was silent for a long moment. "It was a beautiful letter."

"Then did you decide to come here tonight?"

"Yes, I did."

"That's all I really need to know." He laced his fingers between hers and rested their hands on his thigh.

"No, it's not. Tammy Philips came to my office. Her roommate was missing. She hadn't slept in their room the previous night. Tammy needed me as a friend and as a teacher, because she was frightened and didn't know what to do. I couldn't refuse to help her. There's more to being a teacher than teaching classes and reading papers. I wanted to come here, and I wanted to call, but things happened too fast. I wasn't alone until midnight, and then only for a minute."

"Did they find the missing girl?"

She was glad he asked. "Yes. She went off with some boy from the university and had problems getting back. I didn't stay to hear all the details. She's the dean's problem now, and her parents'."

"These aren't little kids you're working with."

"No, but sometimes they still need some support. Tammy did."

"Do you?" It was a solemn question.

"So it seems."

"Is that bad?" He pretended to examine the nails on her captive hand. "Is it so terrible to need me?"

"No, not if you need me."

He laid her hand on his thigh, separating the fingers, his head bowed in silence.

"I'm afraid to tell you how much I need you."

"Adam, I love you!" There was a very good chance she was going to cry again.

He dropped to his knees on the floor and buried his face in her lap, his voice muffled when he finally spoke. "I feel like a disaster survivor."

She knew now what it meant to have feelings overflow. She just couldn't contain all the love she felt for Adam. Dropping to her knees beside him, she closed her eyes and waited for the long, soulful kiss that rocked them both.

"Stay here," he whispered, standing and going to the fireplace.

When he opened the screen, she cried out, "No more books!"

"No." He smiled. "Logs."

She sat on the carpet and watched him stoke up the fire until it was a roaring blaze, safely contained behind the closed screen. Circling around the room, he turned out the light, leaving the room dark except for the fire. Instead of coming back to her, he made his way into the bedroom, returning with a dark bundle, spreading the velvet bedspread and two pillows in front of the fireplace.

"Come talk with me," he said, stretching out with his stockinged feet close to the fire.

Leaving her shoes by the couch, she walked on the edge of the spread, curling her toes on the velvety surface. The fire flamed high, giving their complexions a ruddy hue. She sat beside him Indian style, tucking her heels under her knees, letting her full forest-green wool skirt drop between her thighs. Her white oxford cloth blouse took on an orange hue in the firelight as she traced an embroidered figure on the spread with the tip of her finger.

From where he was lying, he touched her knee, making lazy circles on it with three fingers.

"Did you burn your book of letters?" she asked hesitantly, feeling drained and weak.

"No, I hadn't thought of it yet."

"Your letter was beautiful."

"Not all of it. I was stupid to give an ultimatum and set a time limit."

"Like I did in Maine?"

"Maybe we needed those years apart. I cherish you all the more because of them."

"I love you, Adam." She'd never meant any words so much in her life.

"I love you, Hessie."

He stretched out his arms, and she came to him, cradling her head against his shoulder with her arm across his chest. Contentment was like a sleeping potion, stealing over their happiness and lulling them into a dreamless trance.

Hester awoke first and realized that the gray light of dawn was sneaking around the edges of the drawn drapes. The roaring fire had been reduced to a heap of whitish cinders, and only the warmth of Adam's body kept her from being terribly cold. He stirred beside her, cuddling closer and sighing with happiness.

"I can't believe we slept," she said groggily.

"Just a nap." He aimed for her mouth and missed, sleepily landing a kiss on her chin.

"Adam, I love you."

Her urgency to be believed aroused him. "Oh, baby, I want to believe that."

"Do, then." She wiggled cold fingers under his knit shirt, inching upward from his navel.

"Don't start something you don't want me to finish," he warned.

"Why did we go to sleep last night?"

"A few hours ago, you mean." He pushed her hand away.

"You're still angry because I didn't come sooner?"

"No, darling, no, no, no." He nibbled at her lips but held her hands captive. "I just don't want to make love to you."

"Oh." His rejection stung more than she would've believed possible, and she tried to sit up.

"Wait. I don't want to make love until . . ." His voice trailed off.

"Until what?" She was pouting and didn't care.

"Until you tell me you'll marry me."

"Marry you? You've never asked me!"

"A terrible omission on my part."

"I can't decide on a proposal I haven't heard."

He moved away, stretching his length on the slippery velvet spread and rising to his knees.

"Hester Paine, will you be my wife, in sickness and in health, for better for worse, for richer or poorer, the latter if I don't get over this writer's block and do another book?"

"Until death do us part?" she asked timidly.

"Through all eternity."

"That sounds long enough," she conceded.

Sitting up, she glanced toward the cold embers in the fireplace, not surprised to see her little guardian Puritan women lined up in a row, cheery smiles on every face.

Ye be married soon, Hester.

She blinked her eyes and they faded away, just as she was saying, "Right away."

"I imagine the county building's closed on Saturday," Adam said, "but we can get a license Monday."

"Oh!" She couldn't explain to the man she loved that she hadn't been talking to him. "I didn't mean . . . I mean . . ."

"Did you mean to say yes?" he asked with a teasing gruffness.

"Oh, yes, darling, I did!"

He stood and pulled her up and into his arms, kissing her with deep relish.

"I'm too old to sleep on the floor," he admitted, kissing her again with slow satisfaction.

She glanced toward the hearth a little guiltily, but her tiny Puritans hadn't reappeared.

"It's Saturday and we hardly had a nap last night," she said.

"Is one bedroom going to be a problem?"

"There's lots of space to add on the back of the house

188

when we need more." She unbuttoned her waistband and let the skirt drop to the floor, flipping it aside with her toe.

"Tenure won't interfere with having a little Smith-Woodham, will it?" he asked a trifle anxiously.

"Not with his daddy home to help."

"Daddy works at home!"

"I'll believe that when I see it." She sent her blouse sailing across the room and slowly backed toward the bedroom door.

She laid a trail for him to follow: slip, hose, and bra stretching across the plush carpeting. In the doorway she paused, rolled down her serviceable cotton panties, and dropped them behind her back.

The sleeves of his black turtleneck were like phantom arms reaching across the rug, and his rumpled slacks lay in a bunched-up pile with all his assorted small garments.

"Get the pillows," she said.

"Giving orders before I sign the license?"

"Just a suggestion." She smiled and scampered for the bed, shivering in the chill morning air. The sheets were crisp cotton, and that's the last thing she noticed about his bed for a long, long time.

"We're engaged," she said, testing the sound of it as he slid in beside her. "You're my fiancé."

"For a very short time." He burrowed his head under the covers, tickling her nose with his hair and nuzzling the hollow between her breasts.

"Engaged," she repeated musingly.

He poked his head up and kissed her mouth. "You make it sound like a magic spell."

"It is, in a way. I wasn't sure I'd ever marry." She hugged his shoulders and curled one toe against his hairy leg.

"Darling, you're not even thirty. You hardly qualify as a spinster!"

"Spinster! Your mother would wash your mouth out for using that word." She wiggled to the far side, curling her arms around her knees.

"She wouldn't. My mother believed in progressive child-rearing." He crowded closer, robbing her of the covers.

"That's why you're so spoiled."

"I'm not spoiled! I also have a father who never read Dr. Spock."

He captured her in his arms, grabbing mostly hard knees and elbows, but in the tussle he ended up on his back.

"We really are engaged," she repeated softly.

"Really." He pulled her onto his chest for a no-nonsense kiss that tingled all the way to her toes.

As she leaned over him, her breasts were like fruit ripe for picking, and he fondled them with deceptive gentleness, his lips parting and moving over them while his legs spread in a V, springing together to trap her long, slender limbs.

She could feel the pulse in his neck, hammering against the feathery touch of her lips, and a dancing sensation made her light-headed and ecstatic. His toes teased the sole of her foot, his legs clamped hers, and his hips arched under her weight.

They were on a collision course with the outcome never in doubt, his tongue filling her mouth and his skin on hers arousing a hunger as intense as their love. Without conscious thought, she began to make love to him, dizzily suspended over his body, caressing, pressing, and swaying until every pore was radiating the heat of ecstasy.

Her cries and his moans were a symphony of love, as a great burst of heat engulfed them, making them vibrate as one, united for an incredible consummation. Totally defenseless, she soared to the peak of desire, trembled as skyrockets exploded, and collapsed in throbbing fulfillment, gasping and breathless.

Visions of bathing in hot scented oil and being led to her turbaned master swarmed through her mind, slowly dissolving under the shower of cooling kisses Adam rained on her face and breasts, tumbling her to his side and embracing her with a murmur of delighted gratitude.

"My passionate Puritan," he whispered, glowing with well-being.

She was the conqueror and the conquered, the fierce protector and the tender servant. Very quiet now, she floated slowly back to earth, basking in his loving words and tender touches. For a little while, she hadn't been Hester at all.

"I may not marry you," he whispered.

"Why not?" She was horrified.

"If being engaged to you is like this, I don't want to change anything. You're wonderful just as you are."

"It's you who makes me like this," she whispered against his throat.

"I have something for you." He brushed moist tendrils of flaming red hair from her forehead and kissed her warm brow.

Turning on the light and reaching into a bed-stand drawer, he pulled out a small flat box.

"It's not a diamond. You can help me pick the rings you like. But I've had this too long."

A stone dangled from a fine gold chain, catching the light from the small lamp.

"The opal," she said.

"It can't be unlucky. I've kept it all this time, and now you're with me."

"Maybe it's our special lucky gem."

He leaned over and fumbled with the clasp, hanging the beautiful milky stone with its deep daggers of color around her neck. Moving it to the middle of her throat, he solemnly kissed her lips, then the dark pink nipples below the opal.

"Adam." Her throat felt constricted.

"Darling?"

"I love you so much."

"I can't say it any better than that. I love you, darling, but—"

"But!" She pulled the sheet to her neck and leaned her elbow on the pillow.

"I think we need a marriage contract."

"A contract!" She shot upright, genuinely hurt. "You want a written agreement before we get married?"

"No, putting it in writing isn't necessary. This is going to be a marriage based on trust." He leaned back and watched her with a small smile. "I just don't want my son to be

191

saddled with Smith-Woodham-Paine or Paine-Smith-Woodham. We men have to draw the line somewhere!"

"No more hyphens?" She'd never thought of adding her name to the string he already had.

"Absolutely not!"

"I can agree to that, if . . ."

"If?"

"If you promise to serve me breakfast in bed at least once a week." She found several cozy spots to rest her toes and hands.

"Beginning today?"

"Ummm, that sounds nice. I never had a chance to eat dinner yesterday."

"We'll begin with dessert."

"Dessert for breakfast? That does sound decadent."

"Positively depraved."

His delighted laugh blended with her light tinkle, as he added a postscript to his love letter.